Hunting a Sea-Glass Heart

Renaissance
Diverse Canadian Voices

This is a work of fiction. Any similarity to any events, institutions, or persons, living or dead, is purely coincidental and unintentional.

First edition 2023.

Cover art, design, and typesetting by Nathan Fréchette. Edited by Molly Desson and Shawn Brixi.

Legal deposit, Library and Archives Canada, October 2023.

Paperback ISBN: 978-1-990086-48-9
Ebook ISBN: 978-1-990086-59-5

Renaissance - pressesrenaissancepress.ca

Renaissance acknowledges that it is hosted on the traditional, unceded land of the Anishinabek, the Kanien'kehá:ka, and the Omàmìwininìwag. We vow to use our settler privilege to lift up the voices of our Indigenous hosts and the many marginalized humans who continue to suffer under ongoing colonialism.

Hunting a Sea-Glass Heart

BY

CAROLYN CHARRON

Carolyn Charron gratefully acknowledges the support of the Ontario Council for the Arts.

Renaissance gratefully acknowledges the support of the Canada Council for the Arts.

to my mom, Emily Ramsay
for fostering my love of reading
and being my sounding board whenever I got stuck

to Paul, Renée and Louis
for believing in me even when I didn't

to Emily Elinor—I never forgot

A Funeral

The cloying scent of mourning lilies filled the air around the carved oak casket lying in state in Anne Cormac's drawing room. The perfume clogged in her throat. She looked away from the occupant of the burnished coffin, searching for a distraction. The small fussy tables on either side of the casket with their vases of lilies were useless, as were the family portraits lining the flocked wallpaper and even the view of the gardens beyond the windows.

Remembering the broadsheet she'd discovered in her father's desk that very morning, she carefully slid the paper out of her skirt pocket. It was soft with age and creased almost to breaking. A musty smell wafted up when she unfolded it. She barely recognized her own faded image under the *'Wanted for Piracy!'* caption—she hadn't been that young lass for a good many years.

She leaned over to tuck the folded paper into the dead man's frock-coat. "I kept my promise, Da. I stayed hidden like you wanted. I didn't embarrass you or Jack." She took a deep breath, "But I'm done with hiding now." She half-expected him to sit up in outrage.

For the moment, she was alone with Charles Towne Carolina's preeminent merchant lawyer: her father, William Cormac. The other mourners were on the far side of the house, a silent expanse of wood paneled hall between them. Only the whining of cicadas outside broke the funereal hush of the drawing room.

As she turned away from the casket, a wash of heat swept up her chest, reddening her cheeks and earlobes into a fiery shade that clashed with the lingering auburn of her hair. "Oh, for pity's sake!" Anne muttered. "Not again." The flushing was intense but short-lived, thankfully. She hoped the episodes would disappear entirely once she shifted from maiden to crone.

Tugging at the silly ruffled collar of her dress in a vain effort to cool herself, she hurried away to properly freshen up in private in her own rooms when the truth struck her: she didn't need to hide the flushes anymore. She'd only done so to stop her father's cringes when her womanly curse was brought to his attention.

She opened the door to the grand hall separating the business and private areas of the large house. The murmur of voices in the parlor and formal dining room grew louder. The noise grated at her. The house—her house now—was filled to the rafters with lawyers and merchants, her father's colleagues and neighbors paying their final respects.

Respect. She snorted. They had none. Not one of them had bothered to visit Da as he lay dying these past six months. She resented every syllable of false sympathy dripping from their mouths. If this wake hadn't been one of Da's final wishes, she'd have tossed everyone out on their rumps hours ago. Instead, she wandered the spacious house trying to avoid them, feeling at sixes and sevens. The worse irritation by far was the number of single-minded widowers on the hunt for a wealthy second wife who had appeared among the mourners, all eager to relieve her of managing her father's estate.

A door down the hall opened and the hum of voices grew louder. Swiftly opening the door to her father's study, Anne ducked inside.

A golden glimmer from the sideboard caught her eye—the rum decanter. She splashed a generous tot into a glass, forgoing the water a gentile lady was expected to add. A drink would help her face the hordes again, even if it did encourage those flushes of heat. Her mourning dress of unrelieved black would disguise any resultant wet patches under her arms or elsewhere. She snorted again at the thought of being presentable for the unwanted men in her parlour.

"Miz Anne?" her maid, Sara, poked her head in the door.

"Yes?" Anne snapped, her hand tightening on the crystal tumbler. Turning to the door, she winced at the cautious look on Sara's face. "Forgive me. I shouldn't take my ill temper out on you. It's not your fault all these leeches are here."

"It's quite all right, Miz Anne." Sara grinned at her. "If I took offence easily, I'd never have stayed in your employ." She proffered a stiff parchment, a red blob of sealing wax affixed to one side.

"Impudent lass!" Anne smiled wryly as Sara likely had intended, she'd been smoothing Anne's stormy temper for many years now.

Sara Hughes was something of a rarity in Charles Towne: She was white, and she received a salary. After Jack's birth, Da had insisted Anne have a ladies' maid. Anne had flatly refused a slave—many of her old shipmates and friends had been Black. She'd found Sara, the eleven-year-old daughter of one of her father's legal clients, an Irishman attempting to buy back his bond against the wishes of his owner. She'd raised the lass for more than twenty years now, and they'd become friends along the way.

Anne took the letter from Sara's hand and the maid slipped out, quietly clicking the door shut behind her.

Tucking an escaped lock of white-streaked auburn hair back into her chignon, Anne checked the imprint in the sealing wax holding the parchment closed. The ornately curling W looked faintly familiar and a frown creased her brow as she wondered where she'd seen it before. She cracked the wax open with a soft pop.

The folded parchment blossomed open, leaving a neat square of discoloured paper in the middle. She could see some handwriting half-hidden behind the folded square but she ignored it in favour of the contents first. It was a single page, a creased broadsheet similar to the one she'd tucked into her father's funeral coat earlier. This one was not Anne's own though. The image was that of a man.

Jack Rackham, her beloved Calico Jack, stared out at her from the page.

She caught her breath at the sudden surge of emotions. The last time she'd seen his rakishly handsome face was the day of his hanging. A pang of guilt swept over her—her final words to him had been unkind. Well-deserved, yes, but still unkind.

Putting the broadsheet down, she turned to the crisp parchment used as envelope. There were three lines of neat printing centred on it:

AB,

I know who you are and have stolen your heart.

Meet me where you left your first bastard.

The sweat under her arms turned icy.

AB, Anne Bonny.

Someone knew her true name.

At her father's insistence, she'd kept her identity secret for more than twenty years. She'd gone by her maiden name Cormac, pretending to be her father's daughter-in-law to hide the truth—Jack Jr. was born out of wedlock. She *had* been married but not to Jack's father. To protect her son, she'd have agreed to any condition her father set.

Someone knew who she was, knew whose child was in her belly when Da had ransomed her from hanging. They knew that Jack was the son of two notorious pirates. And mentioning 'her firstborn' meant they knew Jack wasn't her only child with that pirate.

With shaking hands, she downed the shot of rum and splashed another into her glass.

The letter had to be from James Bonny, her erstwhile husband. She'd kill the man if she ever saw him again—it was his doing that Calico Jack, Mary, and the others had been caught. Husband or no, she'd kill Bonny for making Jack lose his father. For making her lose the man who'd claimed her heart after Bonny had broken it.

But what was the heart the letter referred to? Her son Jack was her heart but he was safely in the bosom of the Royal Navy.

With a rush of fear, she suddenly knew the letter was referring to her sea-glass heart. A chunky piece of red sea-glass in the rough shape of a heart, it had been given to her by her other beloved, Mary Read, years ago. It was her most prized possession, being the only memento she had from the best years of her life sailing with her two lovers, Calico and Mary.

Abandoning her second drink, Anne rushed out of her father's office and flew up the stairs to her bedchamber. She yanked open the large drawer of her dressing table and shoved aside the small monogrammed velvet bags containing her jewelry, hunting for the one specially made velvet-lined box where the fragile heart was kept safe.

The tiny carved oak box was empty, the velvet lining still showed the imprint of the irregular chunk of sea-glass.

"God dammit all to hell!" Anne wanted to stab something.

She dashed out of the room, shouting for Sara.

At the bottom of the stairs, Sara walked through the kitchen door, "Calm yourself, I'm here." She stepped lightly despite the large silver tray of hors d'oeuvres in her hands.

"Who left that letter?" Anne demanded.

"I'm sorry, I didn't see who left it. It was with the notes of condolence on the correspondence tray in the front hall," Sara said with a concerned frown, "Is there something amiss? What's happened?"

"I don't know yet. I must puzzle it out first." Leaving the confused Sara to return to their guests, Anne returned to her father's office to stare at the letter.

AB,

I know who you are and have stolen your heart.

Meet me where you left your first bastard.

What did this mean? Her firstborn had Mary's heart? Or someone close to them did. But how? And why? This had the taste of a threat. But was it a threat to her or to her child?

The first time she'd been with child in '18, Anne had agreed with Calico Jack—the sea was no place for a child. She'd given birth in New Providence, now known as Nassau, and Calico had found a family to take the child in. She hadn't regretted leaving the baby behind until after she'd begun raising her son, Jack. But whenever she'd broached the subject of returning to retrieve the child, Da had refused to consider it. Thinking he might soften over time, she pressed him once or twice a year until the year the child would have turned twelve. Jack was nearly nine then and her father's threat to send Jack away to an English boarding school stopped any further attempts.

Calico Jack had left her but a single clue to finding the babe. He'd pressed its tiny footprint onto a clay tablet and scratched the name of the adoptive parents on it. His final words to her had been where he'd hidden the clay tablet—Blackbeard's Well on Mayaguana in the old Pirate's Republic.

She crumpled the threatening parchment in her hand. She had to find the child, grown now but still her firstborn.

She had to go back, back to where it had all started. Her heart leaped with joy at the thought.

A Rebirth

Anne let the memories wash over her. For three glorious years, she'd been part of the *Flying Gang* with her lovers Calico Jack and Mary Read. Until James Bonny had betrayed them to Governor Rogers, and they'd been caught after a late night of carousing.

A brief shiver of guilt passed over her when she recalled her angry last words to Calico: "Had you fought like a man, you'd not be hanged like a dog." A bonny fighter, he and the other men might have fought their way free had they not been pickled in drink. In the depths of her despair at losing him, she'd given her volatile temper free rein and her final words to her love had been angry ones.

Calico and the other men had been hanged in Port Royal. She and Mary had only escaped the noose because they'd pled the belly. Jack had been born a few months after Da had ransomed her back to South Carolina. Then word had come that her beloved Mary had died in gaol along with her babe.

It was time to return to her past, time to find her firstborn child—the baby she and Calico had given up before Jack was born, and before her damned husband could harm either of her children.

Her hands slowly clenched into fists as the old pirate's persona slipped over her like a well-worn cloak, comfortable despite the passage of two decades in silk and lace pretending to be a gentile southern lady. The smell of tar and salt drifted through her mind, and she could almost feel a wooden deck pitching beneath her feet.

She shook off the memories, pleasant though they were, to consider her next moves. With her father gone and her son safe in the Royal Navy, there was nothing stopping her from looking for her lost child at the same time as she hunted down the traitorous James Bonny. She could protect herself and her grown children and get her long-delayed revenge. And if she didn't find any of them, at least she'd be back at sea instead of caged in this mausoleum of a house.

She poured a third tot and tossed the fiery liquid back. Heat rushed up her chest and tinged her ears pink. "Bloody hell, not again." Anne headed down the uncarpeted narrow servants' hall to the summer kitchen for a cold compress while mulling over how to acquire a ship.

She had a few jewels but not enough for even a small vessel. Perhaps she could sell the house. But then what would become of Sara or George? Sara was still young enough to find work as a maid elsewhere, but George was in his dotage and depended on her. She couldn't sell the house. She must find another way to finance a ship.

She snorted with sudden laughter. Was she a pirate or not? She could *steal* a ship. There were at least a dozen plantations lining the nearby Ashley River that received deliveries throughout the year. She would have her pick of vessels.

She'd need a crew. She knew a few of the older men who'd served on pirate vessels and were now at honest work at the docks. One old friend in particular came to mind as a possibility for her first mate: Mortimer McCreary. Between the two of them they would swiftly fill the decks of Anne's new vessel. There was never a shortage of men willing to take a pirate's generous wages.

By the time she arrived at the kitchen still waving the woman's flush away, she was almost dancing with anticipation.

The elderly cook hired for the day took one look at Anne, face and neck rosy pink, and handed her a cold wet cloth. Anne pressed it to her wrists, relieved as the flush began to fade. The kitchen itself was surprisingly cool, since the thick whitewashed walls kept out the worst of the summer heat.

A disheveled Sara bustled into the large kitchen with an empty tray, the gabble of men's voices trailing after her. The noise burst Anne's bubble of excitement. She wanted to be on the move, to find her child, to silence James Bonny if he was threatening to expose her. But she still had a house full of unwanted guests.

The tray clattered onto the long table that dominated the kitchen and Sara picked up another platter of various dainties and cold meats. She gave Anne a weary sigh and went back out to the parlor.

Anne flung her cooling cloth onto the empty tray, tired of hiding from the men invading her house. "I've had enough of men pushing in where they are not wanted. This is my house now, and I want them out." Anne stalked down the hall behind her maid, grinning with anticipation. She'd been restrained for far too long for her father's sake—it was time to cut those apron strings entirely.

Sara used the large tray to nudge the parlor door open with Anne hot on her heels.

"Would you care for a small tidbit?" Sara offered the tray to a small knot of men standing beside the door.

"Depends on the nibble," one of the men said, "I rather fancy something a bit more substantial myself."

Anne saw the younger woman's shoulders stiffen. She felt the same ire rising in her at the man's insulting double entendre.

"Sir?" Sara asked coldly.

"You're a nice little morsel, but with no property you're only worth a nibble or two. I prefer lamb, not mutton, but when the mutton comes with wealth, one must make do."

Shorter than Sara, Anne couldn't see around the maid's back but she recognized the voice. It was Harold Slocam, an old legal partner of her father's and a known letch. He'd been sniffing around Anne for years, although never in her father's unforgiving presence.

"Now your mistress, there's a tasty mouthful if you don't mind getting bit once or twice. Pity she's near useless for breeding now, but the bedding would be amusing," Joseph Burleigh added. Another old partner of her father's, he'd been angry with Anne ever since she'd laughed at his marriage proposal upon her arrival in Charles Towne with a brand-new baby in her arms. His current wife, the third one in twenty years, was a mousy little woman who never spoke above a whisper.

Standing behind her maid, Anne's simmering rage leaped into full boil. She stomped around Sara and into full view of the five men.

As one, they blanched. The youngest, Mr. Slocam's son Hal, actually stepped back until he bumped into the wall with a dull thud.

"Is there something you wish to discuss, *gentlemen?* My father is hardly cold in his coffin, and you are already deciding who shall take me to their bed?" Anne said, her anger barely in check.

The younger Mr. Slocam had the grace to blush, but the others looked down their noses at Anne. None of the five men looked alike nor dressed alike, but there was a similarity to each other; whether they were tall or short, thin or wide, bearded or clean-shaven—the air of condescension and superiority fairly wafted from them. Just seeing them so at ease in her own house made Anne grimace.

The elder Mr. Slocam, Harold, smoothed the front of his fashionable linen frock coat and smirked, "It must be obvious even to you that you must marry now that all your menfolk are gone. It is only natural that there would be interest, despite your age. There are other ways to further one's family line." Slocam ran his eyes down Sara's figure.

"You come to my father's funeral and say this to me? To my maidservant? I have no intention of marrying, especially not to a letch like you." Anne stepped forward until she was inches from his smirking face. Shorter than he by a foot or more, she gave him a cold glare while slipping her favourite dagger from her sleeve. She hadn't used it for years, but it kept its keen edge with no honing.

"You will remove yourself from my presence before I plunge my dagger into your heart," Anne said softly.

The younger Slocam gasped, "Father!"

Slocam looked down and saw Anne's dagger dimpling his fine linen coat directly over his heart. His smirk faded. Anne could see the memory rising in him of the last time she'd used her blade.

It had been years earlier when Jack was still an infant. She'd nearly castrated the man who thought impregnating her without consent would be a fine way to access her father's money. None of the men in the area had been brave enough to try that a second time.

"It's been a long time since my blade has tasted blood. It's hungry." Anne pressed the dagger forward a hairs' breadth. The linen of Slocam's coat popped under the sharp tip.

The acrid stench of urine stained the air, and the portly Slocam stepped back. Stiffly, he nodded and left the room, walking oddly in his dripping trousers. Burleigh and the other men quickly followed. Slocam's son Hal paused for a moment, looking like he wanted to apologize for his father, but a peremptory gesture from Slocam senior pulled him away.

Anne rolled the dagger in her hand and looked out into the large parlor. Sunlight streamed through two tall windows flanking the French doors leading out to the gardens. A dozen or more men stood silent in small groupings along with a handful of brightly clad ladies perched on the settees dotting the floor. As one, the entire roomful of her father's friends and colleagues stared at her and the damply departing Slocam.

"I thank you, gentlemen, ladies, but it has been a very long day and I believe it's time for you to leave." She stroked the blade's length and smiled slightly, allowing just a hint of teeth to show.

Anne marveled at how quickly they moved. The ladies rustled past Anne and Sara in a cloud of costly perfumes and murmured the obligatory expressions of condolences. Their husbands and sons downed the drinks in their hands and abandoned the crystal glasses on the sideboards and tables against the walls before nodding to her as they escaped. Her reputation of having a volatile nature had been the bane of her father's life, but it did come in handy at times like this.

Within a short period of time, Anne and Sara stood alone in the room beside the fragrant puddle on the polished wood floor, listening to the last set of footsteps crunching on the graveled drive.

Anne glanced at Sara, "Good God, I've wanted to do that for years. It was fully as satisfying as I'd hoped."

Sara laughed, joggling the hors d'oeuvres into dancing on the silver tray.

Anne couldn't hold back her own mirth anymore. They laughed even harder when Sara dropped the tray, scattering tiny morsels across the floor and into the puddle Slocam had left, howling until their sides hurt and tears coated their cheeks and the cook came to see what was amiss.

Still holding her aching belly, Anne gasped for breath. It was a great relief to let out the pent-up emotions she'd been holding in for almost a year as she'd tended to her father's illness. She loved her father, truly, but caring for the irascible old man had been a struggle for her temperament.

Saying exactly what she wanted to those disgusting old men who stared at her and Sara as if looking at horses for sale, she felt like herself again. The shackles of polite Southern society had slipped off as easily as a cloak, leaving her lighter.

She lifted the dagger in salute to Sara. The light caught on the roughly engraved initials at the base of the blade.

AB. Anne Bonny. The notorious woman pirate of the *Flying Gang*. The scourge of the high seas for three glorious years.

She'd spent long enough as Miz Cormac, mama of Jack and refined hostess of her good-father's house.

She was Anne Bonny. She would always be that wild Anne. After twenty-odd years entombed on land, she could feel the welcome sway of the deck beneath her feet already.

Chuckling at the image of Slocam pissing himself over fear of her, she tucked the dagger back into its sheath sewn into her sleeve. She'd never stopped carrying a blade hidden some-where on her person—one never knew when a man might need stabbing.

FIRST MATE'S CHOICE

Anne paused in the doorway of The Whore's Blessing, letting her eyes adjust to the dim lighting inside. The mingled scents of spilled beer, fried fish, and urine were thick in the smoky air. The smell brought back a thousand memories of carousing with Calico Jack and the others in Port Royal, south of Jamaica or their home base in Nassau, near the Bahamas. She breathed deeply, pulling the scent into her lungs. Without thinking much on it, she'd dressed for her usual goal of keeping secret her visits here to see her old friends. It was only as she tugged the frayed cuffs of Sara's oldest dress down her wrists as she entered the pub that she realized she hadn't needed the subterfuge. Her father was gone, he would never again deny her seeing her friends.

"Miz Anne! I didn't think I'd see you so soon after your da's funeral." At her entrance, the barkeep looked up from behind the wide counter lining one wall. The rickety unmatched stools lining it were all empty at this early hour, but a double handful of patrons were scattered throughout the room at the equally mismatched tables.

She slapped her hand on the counter, "I didn't let Da keep me from my friends when he was alive, I'll not let his death do it neither. Is McCreary here?"

"In the back, his usual table." He nodded his head towards the back corner and returned to his desultory cleaning.

She strode through the dim room, weaving her way through the tables, greeting a few acquaintances, and smacking a roving hand or two that got a little too friendly with her rear.

"Anne!" a familiar voice called out from the corner furthest from the door.

In the dimness, she made out Mortimer McCreary's bulky figure. A craggy old Irishman she'd known for more than thirty years, Mort had been more than willing to ask around for crew and bring them here today in exchange for a position as her first mate.

"Mort!" She squeezed his bicep in welcome, her hand unable to close around the breadth of it. Despite his age, two decades older than Anne, he was still muscular.

She sat beside him on the rough wooden bench and looked down the long table. Eight men gathered around it, ranging in age from barely old enough to shave to grey-haired like Mort.

"Is tha' Paddy Murray I see?" Anne grinned at the rotund little man sitting on the other side of Mort. "I though' ye was in gaol!" She felt herself slipping back into a thick Irish brogue that matched that of Mort and Paddy. Her father had insisted on proper speech, and it was lovely to let go and speak naturally with her friends.

Paddy laughed, "They lets me out early on 'count of ma good behaviour. Or they gots tired of feeding me!" He patted his belly where it strained the buttons of his shirt. Anne well remembered Paddy's prodigious appetite and his equally large temper. More than one sailor had felt Paddy's boot in their arse. He'd spent at least half his life behind bars for fighting.

"'Tis clear ye havena lost your sense o' humor," Anne grinned again.

"Ah! 'Tis glad I am ta see ye again, Annie. The sea jus' ain't the same wit'out ye."

"I'm right pleased ta see ye too, Paddy."

Mort slid a mug of beer over to Anne. She took a long draught while he pointed across the table to a Black man with a pale hook-shaped scar along his jawline. "Rosso Wilmot."

Anne settled her mug down and nodded at the man. He gave her an impassive look in return.

A skinny fellow beyond Paddy suddenly leaned forward to peer at Anne. "Ya the famous lady pirate?" His thin lips were framed by a beard still patchy with youth.

"Don't know how famous I am but yes, I am Anne Bonny." A flush of warmth filled her—it felt good to reclaim her name.

"Ya don't look like much ta me. My mam's bigger than ya. Ya gots no strength." The youth's lip curled into a sneer.

"Shut yer gob, Lucky," Mort said idly, "Or I'll shut it for ye."

Anne shared a glance with Mort that said, *keep an eye on this one.* She slowly pulled out her bodice knife and began cleaning her nails with the wickedly sharp blade. Without looking at Lucky, she said, "I can hire muscle. Do ye know where the good cargo is or how to get it? No? I do." She cast her eyes around the table, meeting the gaze of each man there. "The King's men think piracy is done. I want ta remind them that we're still here. There's ships just beggin' ta be looted." She didn't mention the search for her firstborn. Only Mort needed that information.

Mugs of beer slammed down onto the table in rough unison. "Hear! Hear!"

Mort grinned and raised his glass to Anne, whispering, "I told ye, ye ain't been forgotten."

A phlegmy cough broke the momentary silence. "Me name is Peg on account I gots one, and this here is Frenchy." The short bald man sitting beside Rosso stuck out a grimy hand for Anne to shake. "You 'n Calico done good for m'brother. I'd consider it a right honour to be on yer crew."

She grasped his paw firmly and searched his weathered face. He was at least fifty but hale and ropy with muscle. "Good to have you. Who was your brother?"

"Andy Baker."

A brief image of Andy swinging on the end of a rope flashed through Anne's mind. "I was that sorry ta see him hanged."

"He had a good life aforehand. Thank'ee, Captain."

Mort waved to the two men on the far side of the table. "That there's Three-fingered Clive and Big Titch."

Clive was a weedy little man who reminded her of her father's accountant, right down to his ink-stained fingers, although Clive only had seven of them. "Quartermaster?" she asked, nodding at his hands.

Clive nodded with a slight smile. "Yes, Captain Anne."

She glanced at his hand, "Why're ye called Three-Finger Clive? Ye got seven."

"The Brits took three, but I ne'er broke 'n tole them where ma Captain was."

Anne nodded soberly. Many a friend had lost fingers or limbs to questioning.

Breaking the solemn moment, Big Titch leaned forward and quirked a gap-toothed grin at her. "I heard ya was looking, and I'm just along for ta ride."

She smiled in welcome at the big man.

Mort pointed to the final man at the table. "Henry's m'choice for sailmaster. He's been on every kind of ship afloat and kin get speed outta them all."

Tall and thin, Henry waved a callused hand at Anne before burying his nose in his mug.

"Paddy's already agreed to be bosun, and if'n Rosso agrees with sail with us, he'll be master o' arms," Mort continued.

Paddy nodded his grizzled head. The curls Anne had so admired years ago hadn't disappeared when he'd turned grey. He'd make a good third mate, Anne thought. Being a stickler for cleanliness and order aboard a ship was essential, and Paddy's immaculately kept nails and clothing showed he was well suited for the job.

Rosso nodded as well, keeping his eyes locked on Anne the entire time. She had the idea that he was scrutinizing her as much as she was the crew. He hadn't agreed to join them yet, making him a clever fellow, perhaps why Mort had him down as weapons master. He'd need to be smart to win a fight and keep the peace within the crew.

Her own job as captain was similar—a pirate ship needed constant balancing between the different personalities aboard. She revelled in the intricate dance between the officers and the common sailors, knowing how much shore leave each needed, how many shares each had earned, and who got the most rum.

In some ways it was similar to the work she'd done for her father when he'd had large dinner parties for his clients and their wives. She'd needed to know minute personal details to keep those parties sailing smoothly too.

She looked down the table and noticed there were faces missing, "Where's Jimbo and Sal? I thought for certain they'd jump at tha chance ta sail again."

"I'm right sorry to say, they're both gone." Mort shook his head, "The lung sickness got 'em both last winter. And I couldna find Hank, Dickie, or Bert neither. I heard they's in gaol, but I wasna gonna go pokin' in there. I gots a few sailors too, but I didn't think ye wanted to meet all o' them lot."

"How about Cookie?" Anne asked, hoping Mort had found him. Cookie had been one of the most sought-after cooks at sea, worth every penny of his two shares.

"The old bastard's alive and kickin'. He'll join us next week, gotta get himself out o' a situation first."

"A situation? What's he done?"

"Nothin' 'gainst the law. He's chef down ta Governor Johnston's house." Mort scratched his head.

"He took a job? A legal job? With a Scotsman ta boot?" Anne chuckled and slapped her knee. "Well, ain't that a kick in tha arse." The half-Irish Cookie had always said that any Scotsman was a devil sent to plague him.

"Taking a job beats starving," Henry said quietly, "even with a man you hate."

Most of the heads nodded around the table, including Anne's. A small silence fell over the table as they remembered people they'd lost to starvation. The sounds of the other patrons were a quiet murmur in the background.

Anne raised her glass in a silent tribute to Calico, Mary, and all the others she'd lost and took a long draught of her beer. She wiped the foam from her lip then said, "Ye've all read and signed tha code?" She and Mort had drafted it a few days earlier. The code outlined the various rules and punishments for breaking them as well as share allocation, compensation for injuries and the like.

Again, everyone nodded. Except Rosso.

Mort eyed him, "Ye'll have to sign it afore I kin give ye any shares."

Rosso gave Anne a long look, then turned to Mort, "I'll sign when we're aboard."

Mort glanced at Anne who shrugged slightly before he nodded slowly to Rosso.

"Well then, it looks like all we need now is a ship." Anne smiled, "And I know just tha place ta get one." She felt a flush rising in her cheeks and took a quick sip of her beer to cover it.

"'Course ye do!" Mort raised his glass, "ta Cap'n Anne!"

In the chorus of cheers that followed, only Anne heard Mort's whispered words. "Did ya talk to Benji?"

She patted her breast pocket where a paper crinkled. It contained a short list of ships and routes. "He's just like his da," she grinned, "willing to share his information for a share." The son of another old sailing mate, Benji would never be an official member of her crew, at least not one that went to sea with her. He was too valuable in his position as assistant harbourmaster.

Mort grinned and tapped her mug with his own. "'Course he is! Who wouldna want ta join wit' Cap'n Anne, Scourge o' the High Seas?"

Feeling eyes on her, Anne looked across the table at Rosso's serious face. He wasn't quite convinced yet. Yes, definitely a smart man she wanted to have on her side; Mort had chosen her new crew wisely.

She winked at Rosso and was rewarded with a soft smile that didn't quite reach his eyes. It was early days yet, but she hoped he made the right decision about her.

It would be a pity to have to kill him just after meeting him.

Leave-taking

"**S**ara, have you seen my boots?" Anne called out from the depths of her wardrobe. There was a jumble of shoes and boots littering the cupboard floor, but not the ones she was looking for, a pair of ancient leather boots perfectly broken-in to the shape of her feet.

An owl's hoot came from beyond the open window. Anne lifted her head to listen. Superstition said that an owl's cry was a harbinger of death, but she didn't believe it. She'd always found them to be good luck. A warm breeze brushed across her face bringing with it the scent of fresh mown grass.

"They're in the pantry, Miz Anne!" Sara dragged another case bump, bump, bump down the front stairs.

Anne ran lightly down the back stairs and scooped up the knee-high boots from the tiled floor of the pantry, not questioning why her boots would be in such an unlikely place—Sara's idea of housekeeping was unique. It was fortunate that there was a housekeeper to oversee the house's affairs, or Anne was certain all her belongings would soon be lost.

Stamping her feet into the boots, she hurried up to the front hall to pose for Sara in the lamplight. "How do I look?"

"Positively piratical, Miz Anne!" Sara was one of the few people who knew of Anne's past. Anne had disclosed her secret a few years earlier in a rare moment of tipsy openness. Sara's bright eyes and eager questions had led to hours of conversation since.

Anne twirled with a quick flourish of the sash she'd wrapped about her waist. It had taken some hunting to find her old clothing—Da had buried them deep in the attic where they disappeared behind years of accumulated detritus. Fortunately, the loose fit meant no alterations were needed. She didn't have the tiny waist she'd once had; birthing two babes had changed her figure from girl to matron.

However, being matronly also meant none would expect her to fight. She planned to use that to its full advantage in her mission. She had not forgotten how to swing the cutlass hanging at her side nor how to use the daggers tucked into her cleavage, sleeves, and boot-tops.

"I must be off. I'm sorry I can't take you with me." Anne eyed the younger woman, half expecting Sara to begin her argument anew.

"I'll stay behind," Sara said a touch sulkily for a grown woman, "Don't forget your promise to take me out when you return in a few weeks."

"Even if the weather holds and the wind blows fair, it may be more than a month." Anne cautioned, then gave Sara a questioning look. "You understand why I can't take you now?"

"I do. I must pretend you are in seclusion, mournin' your father, and I cannot do that if I'm not here to turn away the occasional guest." Sara said and then sighed. "I'll keep packin' up your father's things as you asked. I wish you'd reconsider. What will the neighbours think? He's barely cold in his grave."

Anne ignored Sara's comments. If—when—she returned, she'd be expected to move into her father's rooms, and she had no intention of using the heavy dark furniture Da had favoured. It was best to wipe the rooms clear of his presence and start afresh. If she returned for more than a day or two at all.

She stroked her hand down the indigo sash around her waist, remembering the feel of a deck beneath her feet. The search for her lost child was the professed reason she was returning to the sea, but now that her departure was imminent, Anne realized how much she yearned to go back—the salt in her veins throbbed with eagerness. With her father buried and her son settled into adulthood in the arms of the Royal Navy, the last of the bonds holding her to land were shredding into mist.

Sara cleared her throat, bringing Anne back to the tiled foyer where they stood amidst the packed crates of her father's things. A rough sackcloth bag was puddled atop one of the wooden boxes. Her supplies, Anne assumed. She'd asked for her personal items to be readied: her monthly rags and under-garments along with an extra coin purse and the framed miniature of her son.

"I'll send a few men to pick up the supplies stashed in the barn as soon as I have the ship well in hand. You keep an eye out that George doesn't see those particular crates."

"I gave him a dose of laudanum in his dinner—he'll sleep 'till mornin'." Sara grinned at Anne.

Startled, Anne blinked, then chuckled. "You are far too much like your mistress."

Sara laughed, her good humour restored. "How many of your old crew did you find?" She fiddled with the strings holding Anne's pack tightly closed.

"Not many. Nearly twenty who escaped the noose. Another six will join us in Nassau. We may even find a few turncoats among the *Woolford's* crew." The *Woolford* was the supply ship Anne had chosen to be hers. The two-masted sloop was a regular visitor to a nearby plantation and frequently docked for days at a time. Two days ago, it had anchored downstream and now unknowingly awaited Anne's liberation. As a narrow-hulled sloop, the ship would be agile, and with two masts, it would be steady in the roughest weather. But the deciding factor was the *Woolford* had five cannons, all six-pounders, two per side and one movable on the weather deck. When she'd last been at sea, only the Navy had such rich armament.

"Do you truly think you can take the ship with only old men?" Sara plumped herself down on one of the metal-strapped trunks of Anne's father's suits.

"With the blunderbusses and muskets I've given them? They need only remember how to aim. None of the crew will be ready to fight, much less use their cannon to any effect." Anne expected little resistance—there hadn't been a reported pirating along the Carolina coast in years, so tonight's events would be unexpected—and she'd specifically hired sailors who were experienced fighters, even if some of them were a little long in the tooth.

She thought on the younger officers, Henry and Rosso. Henry Lissome was their youngest officer, only 38 years of age but well-versed in sail management. She knew nothing of his weapons training and made a mental note to ask Mort.

Rosso Wilmot was near her own age. His extensive training with blades and ranged weapons such as cannons and bows was the reason he was weapons master. Mort had spoken very favourably on his proficiency.

At least half of the dozen sailors who would fight this night were well seasoned so Anne's lack of practice and Henry's possible inexperience shouldn't be a problem.

Sara sighed. "I will miss you."

Anne tucked her distinctive red hair into a dark blue kerchief and smiled at Sara's reflection in the hall mirror. "I'll be back soon, and you can join me for a short sail before we have to scuttle the ship," Anne promised, although she wasn't sure she'd be able to make herself sink the vessel at all. Once she'd tasted being at sea again, would she be able to give it up a second time?

Slinging the musket strap over one shoulder and the cloth bag over the other, Anne strode down the graveled walk to the stables where her horse waited for the short ride to the next plantation where her prey floated at anchor.

The early September heat surrounded her, and cicadas whined in the dark. The sound had been one of Jack's favourites. More than once, Anne had heard him making a buzzing noise while at play with the neighboring lads. A lump filled her throat at the thought of her son—she hoped she would be home before his next shore leave. It would be terrible to miss a visit; they were so rare.

The cicadas grew quiet as she rode her horse along the rough road and resumed their chorus when she moved on. Anne wondered if her firstborn liked them too, although she couldn't quite remember if there were cicadas in Nassau.

Twenty years was a long time to remember such inconsequential details.

Had the child been a lad or lass? She'd asked Calico to take it away before she'd learned, and he'd kept his counsel for years after. Perhaps if he'd lived to see Jack born, he'd have told her then.

She knew nothing about her firstborn, whether the child had lived past babyhood, whether Calico made provisions for it. She wanted to learn everything she could. Even if she discovered the worst, she could at least lay flowers on the baby's grave. She wished she could do the same for Calico, but she had no idea where his body lay or if it had been given to the sea. She'd joined Mort and the others in the pub a few years later to raise a glass to their lost friends, but there'd been no pirate funeral for Calico. Being full of pageantry and speeches, and copious drinking of course, pirate funerals were great fun for the mourners. She'd always felt a touch guilty over not giving that send-off to Calico or Mary.

The liquid slapping of water on the underside of a dock broke into her thoughts, and she reined the horse to a halt.

Bushes and trees loomed out of the darkness. They lined both sides of the dirt road leading to the weathered dock ahead. The *Woolford* was anchored a short distance offshore, and her men would be close by, keeping watch. Glancing over her shoulder, she checked the moon's position and dismounted.

"Over here, Cap'n Anne." Mort's distinctive drawl came softly from the deeper darkness a few paces away.

Her boots made little sound on the grassy strip beneath the trees as she made her way to Mort's voice. The smell of sweat, faint but acrid, wafted to her from the men standing in a clump with Mort. She couldn't quite make out how many stood there. Only the rustle of leaves as they occasionally moved betrayed their presence.

She looped her reins to a tree set back a distance from the road's verge.

"Everything's set?"

"Aye, lass," Mort said.

Anne suppressed her displeasure at Mort's disrespectful address. They had a battle ahead of them; this was not the time.

The men stretched out in a ragged line and began creeping up the road to the dock. One shadow came closer to Anne and whispered, "Mort asked me ta fight alongside ya as needed." She recognized Rosso's deep voice.

Mildly annoyed by Mort's assumption she needed a guard, particularly one she hadn't yet given her full trust to, she nodded. "Let's go then."

Blood thundered in Anne, filling her with energy. Swinging at a practice target was never the same as at a live man. She remembered the red haze that took over her entire body, adding force to each blow.

"Stay out o' range o' my blade," she whispered, "'tis hard to see a friend in the dark."

"Especially one with ma dark skin," Rosso laughed quietly.

Anne couldn't help laughing with him. She always did appreciate a sense of humour in a man. Her opinion of the man ticked up a notch.

Taking the Woolford

The ship bobbed a distance offshore, a dimly-lit rounded shape in the dark. The fore and aft lanterns glinted off the water. A flat-bottomed barge was snugged up to the end of the floating dock, ready to take cargo ashore as soon as daylight came. All twenty-two of the men with her would fit on the barge, but it would be impossible to hide the barge's movement from the night crew aboard the *Woolford*. They needed a more subtle approach.

Anne whispered to Mort. "Y'all set? Remember, stealthy approach, don't give 'em any time ta prepare a defence."

Mort shook his head—he had no liking for a midnight swim. He waved a leathery hand to Rosso. "I ain't swimmin', he is."

Anne gave Mort a look of unspoken concern, and he nodded gravely to indicate he stood by his assertion that Rosso could be trusted to not betray them. She nodded back to him—she trusted Mort with her life, so she would give Rosso the benefit of the doubt.

Rosso's shoulders were broad like a blacksmith's and as heavily muscled. He flashed a grin at her before he skinned out of his faintly luminescent white shirt and dove into the water without a sound. Within a few feet, he disappeared in the inky waves. Anne smiled a little remembering his quip about being invisible in the dark.

"Ten minutes," someone whispered, "Who'll bet me?"

Anne shushed them; sound carried a long way over water. She peered out into the darkness, waiting for the signal.

Less than a quarter hour later, a lamp flickered over the side of the ship and dipped up and down twice before returning to its usual spot along the rail. Anne glanced at Mort. They would soon learn if Rosso was the man Mort thought he was.

"Get aboard, quickly now," Mort muttered. The men and Anne slipped out of the bushes and filed onto the barge. Two crewmen silently poled out to the ship where Rosso had dropped the rope ladder down the side.

"Leave yer boots in tha barge, ijiit, we don' wan' no noise," Mort hissed at Lucky as he stood up.

Lucky and two others sat back down to remove their shoes while the older men, already barefoot and rolling their eyes at the greenhorns, began the climb. A young man at each end of the barge used padded poles to prevent it bumping into the side of the vessel—the booming would surely wake the sleeping crew.

One by one, the crew climbed up until Anne was the last. With her first touch on the rough rope ladder, the pirate who had begun to emerge with her change of clothing roared fully to life, shrugging off the last vestiges of the widow and mother persona she'd worn like an ill-fitting dress.

The smell of salt and the bitter tang of tar coating the ship's timbers was thick in her nostrils. Step by step, she scaled the swaying ladder, her excitement for the upcoming battle growing until it felt as if her skin would burst with it. By the time she leaped over the railing, her focus was razor-sharp for the skirmish at hand, every sound and scent crystal clear in the dark.

Rosso waited for her at the railing. The only thing she could hear on deck was the soft breathing of twenty barefoot and sweaty men spoiling for a fight.

Nearly under her feet was a corpse, a cord still embedded deeply in its throat. Rosso's work. The weight of uncertainty left her shoulders: he could be trusted.

Mort raised his hand and looked at her. She drew her cutlass from her sash and nodded once, curtly.

Instantly the entire group dispersed to their assigned stations. After giving them a moment to take a deep breath and prepare for the work ahead, Anne cleared her throat loudly, the signal to start.

The two hatches were flung open loudly and two thirds of Anne's men dropped below decks into the crew quarters and holds, screaming for blood.

Anne, with Rosso close beside her in the final group, stormed the captain and officer's cabins under the wheel deck.

She burst through the captain's door directly behind Mort. A guttering lamp hanging over the desk barely lit the interior. In the dim room, all she could see was a pair of naked buttocks pumping energetically on the bunk. Under the pasty shoulders of the grunting man, a pale woman's face lay on a pillow, streaked with tears.

Mort swung his blade and knocked the fellow flat onto the woman. Blood spurted from a shallow slice across the naked man's lower back.

Pushing Rosso to the side, Anne screamed and swung her cutlass, scoring a second red line across the officer's shoulders.

The naked woman beneath him shoved hard, tumbling him to the deck to splay face-up, his frightened eyes darting from person to person. She leaped to her feet and snatched up the sheathed dagger hanging from a peg on the wall, then spun on her bare heel and crouched over the stunned man. "Go t'hell, ya vicious bastard," she growled and plunged the dagger into his eye. Blood bubbled up from the puncture and washed down his cheek as he relaxed into death.

Crouched over the body, the naked woman looked up. Her wide-eyed gaze tracked from Rosso to Mort to Anne, the dripping blade clutched in her fist, blood and bruises streaking her body from shoulders to hips.

"'Tis fine, we're not gonna hurt you," Rosso said softly, holding his hand out, whether for the dagger or in entreaty, Anne couldn't tell.

The woman dropped the dagger onto the dead man's chest, then stood and plucked up a threadbare cotton dress from the floor and pulled it over her head before turning to face them again. Her eyes widened when she realized Anne was a woman.

"You'd be welcome to come with us," Anne said, her voice gruff.

The woman looked away from Anne, "Cain't leave wit'out m'baby. 'Sides, I ain't a sailor." She looked at Anne's worried face and added, "They ain't all as bad as 'im." She stepped over the dead man and scooped up the money pouch on the desk with a faint clink. "Ma earnings for tonight."

"Of course. If... if any trouble comes from tonight... if you need help, go to the Cormac house up the west road. Tell the lass there that Anne Bonny sent you."

The woman nodded, but her eyes were still wary, and she moved sideways through the crowded room as if afraid she would be stopped.

Watching her go, Anne wished they'd been just a few minutes earlier. She glanced at the dead man's uniform jacket on another wall peg before following Mort and Rosso above deck.

By the time she reached the main deck, the ship was secure. Other than the foc'sle guard that Rosso had strangled, there had only been three sailors and two more junior officers asleep below decks. A single prisoner stood beside Henry, a turncoat possibly. The rest of the crew must have been ashore, including the captain, the jacket belonging to the dead man in the cabin bore the pips of first mate.

Anne pulled her boots out of the jumbled pile one of her men had tossed on deck and tugged them on while watching the men rushing around on Mort's orders.

He'd assigned the four brawniest men to bring the bodies up on deck. Once the others met them upstream with the supplies they'd gone ashore to fetch from Anne's barn, they would head out to sea where the bodies would be slung over the rail. In the meantime, the cabins and decks must be swabbed down before they began to reek.

Breathing hard with the aftermath of fighting, Anne watched the prostitute sitting regally in the stern of the barge while four of Anne's men poled it ashore. She knew all too well the life that awaited the woman ashore. It could easily have been her own life if not for Da's wealth to protect her.

Shaking off the thought, she turned to Henry's prisoner, "Give me a reason ta trust ya won't turn on me."

Even in the lamp-light, she saw the prisoner blanch under his deep tan.

"I can't." His voice shook a little, "But I give you my word that I won't."

She studied him. "What's yer name?" He was sturdy and looked strong, although he wasn't yet full grown.

Perhaps three decades younger than herself, he was scared but met her eyes squarely. "Brian, Cap'n, Black Brian on account of my hair."

"Don't make me regret this."

Rosso cleared his throat, "I'll speak for him, Cap'n."

She studied Rosso's face in the flickering lamplight. He hadn't betrayed them, but she still didn't have the full measure of the man. "Are you sure you want ta tie yer fate ta a stranger?" she said at last.

Rosso nodded, "Ya did the same for me. I might ha' warned the *Woolford* crew and ambushed ya."

She gave him a long searching look. Mort hadn't overestimated his intelligence; he'd said as much when he'd suggested who should swim to the ship. "All right then. He's yer responsibility until he proves himself trustworthy." She turned away.

Alone for a brief moment, amidst the scurrying sailors readying for departure, her eyes ran the full length of the merchant ship.

The brass fittings glimmered in the lamplight, as did the well-scrubbed decking. The water lapped softly along the sturdy wooden timbers. She was a pretty vessel—fair lines, reefed sails, and everything shipshape.

The red haze of battle was fading, and a new feeling grew in its place in Anne's belly: pride of ownership.

This was her ship now. Her first solo command.

Grinning, she strode to the wheel deck above the officers' quarters and bounded up the six steps. With the first touch of her fingertips to the cool wood of the steering spokes, she felt twenty years of land-locked life as Anne Cormac, mother and widow, drop away to vanish in the dark water below.

Anne stroked the smooth wheel and felt the river shifting beneath her, cradling her in its embrace. A few hours sailing upriver and she would be at sea.

Anne Bonny, Pirate Captain, would be home at last.

Anne's Revenge

Anne's hips ached from the vigorous fight. She rubbed one spot surreptitiously to ease the pain. She knew she'd feel the rheumatism much worse after she'd slept a while. She hoped it never got as bad as her father's. He'd been barely able to walk some mornings. She'd asked Sara to add a fair bit of dried willow bark into her personal belongings. She didn't want the crew to know her hips ached, and willow bark tea helped.

Movement below her on the weather deck caught her eye. A scuffling sound came from the portside ladder as the crew scrambled aboard and swiftly lowered ropes to pull the supplies up from the barge. An hour's sail upriver, they'd pulled ashore at an unmarked beach just after dawn to pick up the rest of their stashed supplies and three additional crew members. There was no sense to showing themselves in Charles Town port to pick up supplies and having someone remember them.

The flickering lamplight was nearly drowned out by the rising sun, but it illuminated the port railing in the shadows where a group of men took the supplies off the plank lift and distributed them to sailors with directions for where to put it. Three of those who stood waiting were strangers recently hired by Mort. One in particular caught Anne's eye—a slender figure standing with a barrel balanced on one hip listening to instructions.

She eyed the figure suspiciously, something about the person seemed odd. She suddenly remembered where she'd seen that particular pose before. She'd seen plenty of men carrying barrels, but she'd only seen one woman; her friend and lover Mary Read. Men didn't rest heavy loads against their hips that way. Mary had. Anne did it herself.

This was no lad standing before her. *She* was a lass. The question was why she'd felt the need to hide. If any place was safe for a lass in a man's world, it was on a pirate ship—especially one captained by a woman.

She stepped up to the lass. "You. My cabin. Now." She headed for the captain's quarters without turning to see if the lass followed.

The sailor was white-faced with fear when she stepped through the door, letting it shut quietly.

Anne stood behind the captain's desk, arms crossed over her chest. "I know you're a woman. What's your true name?"

"Alexandra Cunningham," the lass whispered hoarsely.

"Giv' me one reason why I shouldna throw you o'erboard." Anne withdrew her dagger from the scabbard hanging at her left side and gently laid it onto the desk between them.

Alexandra's gaze followed it down. She swallowed hard but stood her ground. "I... just wanted to get onto a crew. No one else would take on a woman. I thought you'd be the same."

"I see. You thought a woman captain wouldna like another woman on board." Anne raised an eyebrow, "Did your parents raise any intelligent children?"

The lass's lips tightened. Whether in anger or embarrassment, Anne didn't know.

"I..." Alexandra began.

"Every word out of your mouth from now on will be the truth. Or you will be shark bait." There was something familiar about the shape of the lass' tight jawline, Anne thought while waiting for an answer.

"Yes, ma'am." Alexandra looked down, audibly grinding her teeth, her fingers drumming nervously on her thighs.

"Does Mort know your true name?"

"No, ma'am."

Anne sighed heavily, "Captain. Not ma'am. Well, I'll not go against Mort hiring you even if he thought you were a lad, but I hope for your sake that you're a quick study." She eyed the young woman consideringly. "Can you read and write?" After the lass nodded, she continued, "Go and ask paint and a brush from Rosso. The *Woolford* needs a new name. *Anne's Revenge* has a nice ring to it." The first vessel she'd sailed on as a full-fledged pirate had been the *Queen Anne's Revenge,* her old friend Blackbeard's ship. The abbreviated name seemed a fitting tribute to all her old companions and to her current quest.

Alexandra nodded and dashed out the door, bare feet slapping on the wood.

"Mort!" Anne called through the open door while taking a considering glance around her cabin. The leather topped desk bolted to the floor dominated the small room. It was large enough to be used to plot their course on the oversized maps. A single chair, also bolted to the floor, was the only seating in the room. Behind the desk, flush against the curved outer wall was a polished oak cabinet where the captain kept the maps and, hopefully, a personal supply of rum. At the far side of the room a generous bed was built into the space below the casement window in the stern wall. A blanket spilling from the bed partially hid the six drawer fronts below the mattress. All of the immaculate brass hardware on the cabinet and bed gleamed in the soft light from the hanging lamps over the bed and desk.

There was very little floor space for another person to sleep in this room, but Anne couldn't leave the lass with the crew or she'd be with child very quickly. "The lass will have to make do with the floor in front of the desk." Anne shrugged, dismissing it.

Mort poked his head in from examining his own quarters across the narrow passageway. "Lass?"

"Bring me Alexandra's bedroll. She'll bunk here with me."

"Alex... andra?" His eyes widened a fraction in his weather-beaten face.

Anne nodded, "S'up to you if you want to tell the others, but I figured you needed to know as you'd hired her." She raised an inquiring eyebrow.

"Damn my eyes! I knew there were somethin' off with tha lad... lass. Sorry Cap'n." Mort's head disappeared, and she heard him bellowing for a sailor to run and fetch Alex's things.

Plucking her dagger from the desk, she studied it for the hundredth time, running her thumb gently over the edge. Someday she would find the blacksmith who'd created it—she'd never had a blade keep so keenly sharp without needing constant honing. There was a maker's mark on the base of the blade almost hidden by the hilt, the initials EB, but she had no other way of tracing the blacksmith.

Shaking her head to dispel the distraction, she tucked the dagger back into her sash then slipped her coat off and rolled up her sleeves. She'd spent enough time on distractions; she had plenty of work to do before they could begin their quest. Whether her child was dead or alive, she was determined to find the clay tablet hidden so long ago by Calico Jack. It was the first step to learning who had her sea-glass heart and whether they were a threat to her and her family.

Anne pulled out the previous captain's log book from its shelf in the cabinet and eased herself into the chair, grateful to be off her aching hips. She flipped to the last page of the log book to begin reading the most recent entry.

A gentle tap on her open door broke into Anne's thoughts.

She didn't bother looking up from plotting their route to the Bahamas. A final beam of evening light caught on the rum bottle holding down one corner of the chart, while her boot held down another. "Enter."

Alexandra limped into the captain's quarters. "Captain, I've finished."

Anne grunted. The breeze from the open window stirred the papers on the desk, leaving a salty tang on her lips. They'd moved far enough out to sea during their day's sail that they could barely see the coast. And now that the bodies had been tossed over the rails, the stench of corruption was gone, leaving nothing but the clean sea breeze.

From the corner of her eye, Anne saw the young woman

wince and swallow every time the ship rocked on the swells. There was a green tinge to her face. "Bloody balls in a sack! Are you seasick?"

"I am not." The muscles tightened along Alex's jaw.

"You are the most foolish child I have ever had the misfortune of meeting. Why on earth didn't you say something? Cookie has herbs to help you get your sea legs."

"I'm not seasick, it's my monthlies, and I'm hungry! And I'm not a child. I'm nearly twenty-three." A loud rumbling came from her belly, punctuating the young woman's words.

"How is it that you missed mess?" Anne peered up at the young woman.

"Because no-one pulled me up," Alexandra growled, "They left me hanging over the side all day, no matter how much I called out. One of the idiots even pissed over the side aiming for my head."

Anne snorted with laughter. The crew must already know that Alexandra was a woman—Anne remembered her own rough treatment when she'd been uncovered. "Go see Cookie. He'll give you something to eat."

"Aye, aye, Captain." Alexandra looked down and a puzzled frown creased her forehead when she saw her duffle beside Anne's desk. "That's my bag. Why..." she blanched but managed to stop a hair short of questioning her captain.

"You'll sleep on the floor in here. No sense riling up the crew with another woman they can't play blanket hornpipe with." Anne snickered at the blush rising in Alexandra's cheeks at the crude joke. "Didn't I just tell you to see Cookie? Why are you still here?"

Alexandra immediately spun and dashed out, exposing the back of her neck which was a bright angry red under her raggedly shorn hair.

"And get something for that sunburn!"

She suddenly remembered how badly Calico had sunburnt. He'd worn colourful cotton neckerchiefs to stop their mates from laughing at his bright red neck—the material that had given him his nickname of Calico. She shook her head and went back to her papers, washing her hands of the lass's fate. Alexandra would either toughen up or be tossed overboard by her own actions.

Anne pushed aside the charts to peruse the cargo manifest, hoping that they wouldn't need to make a supply run and could head straight to Mayaguana. She was happy to see a wide variety of goods in the main hold, textiles and foods mostly. Including a number of live turtles.

Cookie would be thrilled. Anne was not fond of turtle soup, but turtles made less mess than goats or sheep and wouldn't go wormy like barrels of salted beef or taste fishy like eels. The crew would be delighted to have a dish usually reserved for the wealthy.

Anne let out a whoop of glee at the next entry, sixty-four barrels of Watling rum. Watling was Anne's preferred brand of tipple. By weight alone, it was worth more than gold.

This explained the *Woolford*'s recorded route from Jamaica to Charles Towne, followed by New York, then back to England: rum was her main cargo.

Abandoning the maps on the desk, Anne ransacked the built-in cabinets until she located the previous owner's personal stash. "Much obliged, Captain Kenlock!" The bottle holding down the map on her desk was drinkable, but only barely. She'd snagged it from the sailors' mess earlier in the day. She held the hidden bottle of rum up to the light to critically eye the colour before she sniffed the contents. She poured herself a small glass and took a lingering sip. The alcohol burned a path down her throat and set her cheeks to flushing again.

Anne waved the woman's heat away and returned to rifling through Kenlock's papers in the cabinet, one drawer at a time. She'd already gone through the drawers under the bed and found a truly remarkable quantity of clothing. Apparently, Kenlock had been something of a dandy. She'd have to get one of the crew to disperse the lot of it. Except the captain's coat and hat of course. They'd be a handy disguise.

From outside the open door, the sweet sounds of Silver Tongue's voice drifted in. She recognized a pumping shanty and paused in examining the papers to listen for a moment. Mort had done well in finding them a shanty man. The Black man's voice was truly a treasure, as a good voice made the tedious task of pumping out the bilges almost enjoyable.

A folded piece of parchment atop the pile in the next drawer made her laugh with delight. It was a letter of marque—a wonderful find. It gave them official permission to take anything they wished from England's enemies at sea, whether men or goods. In short, they could appear as legal privateers.

Anne grinned. She didn't need permission to take what she wanted, but this would prevent them from being charged with piracy and sent to gaol or the gallows. Pirate or privateer, *Anne's Revenge* was ready for glory and fortune.

That's the Way the Cookie Grumbles

Cookie stomped his way up the six steps to the wheel deck. "Ta flour's gone ta weevils and ta goat's done died on me."

Standing at the tiller, Anne raised an eyebrow. Cookie was disheveled and unshaven. Apparently, he'd spent the last two days grubbing about in the gallery's storeroom. "Ye'll have to make do for a few more hours. We board 'em tonight." Their man in the Charles Towne harbour, Benji, had given her a list with six likely prospects for plunder, all of them along their current route to the Bahamas—the first stop in her journey to find her child and her stolen heart.

"If'n I have ta." He wiped the sweat from his balding head with the end of his bright red sash and stomped back down below. "But I ain't happy ta wait."

Anne winced, she hoped she wasn't going to pay for his displeasure with overly spicy food. Or weevil-filled biscuits. She'd have to be mighty hungry to eat those.

Mort poked his head up from his reclined position on the ropes coiled behind her. "That man sure do love ta complain."

"Unless you want him to spit in your food, I'd be quiet if I were you," Anne snorted and spun the wheel one notch eastward.

"Nah, we're old mates. He spits in ma food already." He squinted into the sun a few degrees off the portside. "We'll catch 'em 'round ten o' the clock, I reckon." He was referring to their current target, a small black dot in the endless blue of the ocean ahead of them.

"Can we hurry up a mite, Henry?" Anne called over the railing in front of the wheel, "We wanna catch 'em just at dark."

"Aye, aye!" Henry passed on the orders.

Mort pulled out his pipe and tobacco pouch. Thumbing the bowl full, he peered up at Anne. "Why're ye so cantankerous? I ain't never seen ye like this afore a battle."

Anne sniffed, "Don't know what ye mean. And put tha' damned pipe out."

"Ye act like ye wanna be someplace else. Is there sumpin' I should know 'bout?" He puffed on his pipe for a moment, blithely ignoring her command to put it out.

Briefly, she considered telling him more about why their next stop after their first plunder would be Nassau, but she was too used to keeping her own counsel. She'd spent years of pretending her father was her father-in-law and she a respectable widow. "No. Merely looking forward to meeting our new suppliers."

"Suppliers." Mort laughed. "Ye do have a winnin' way with words, lass."

"Enough with the 'lass'." Anne scolded him. "I'm your captain now."

"True enough, but 'tis hard ta stop a habit o' twenty years." He puffed smoke in her direction.

"If you got nothin' better ta do than bite my arse, you can take over tha tiller, and I'll find somethin' else." She glared at him before checking the octant to confirm their heading. "Tha wheel's yours. And I told ye to put that damned pipe out!" She threw the words over her shoulder as she descended the short ladder with Mort's amused chuckles following her.

A vigorous rapping on her door woke Anne from a nightmare of chasing after Jack and his faceless sibling and over and over watching them disappear into fog, fall into gaping pits, or be lost overboard.

Soaked in sweat, she sat up, relieved to be awake. "Yes?"

The door latch snicked open.

"Cap'n Anne, we's almost there. Mort needs you on the bridge." Little Titch's still childish voice cut through the gloom.

"What time is it?" Her voice was raspy with sleep, and she could still faintly taste the rum she'd tossed down earlier.

"Nine o' the clock. Sun's just above the horizon."

"Tell Mort I'll be there directly."

"Aye, Cap'n Anne." He carefully placed a dark lantern on her desk, far away from the rolled maps in their wooden box attached to the floor. The lantern's shutters were almost closed, letting only a little light escape.

As soon as the door shut behind Little Titch, Anne clambered to her feet and staggered over to the liquor cabinet.

She chugged a mouthful of rum straight from the bottle and shuddered.

"Damnation." She shook her head, dispelling the lingering dreamy horror of watching her son plunge to his death hand in hand with his brother or sister. Plucking up her pistol belt, she strapped it around her waist. Even though she'd checked them before laying down to rest, she checked them again in the dim light. She blew the light out and left her quarters.

It was shadowy up top with both the fore and aft lanterns shuttered. The sun was nearly below the horizon, and long shadows filled the space between the lanterns. She passed a couple of sailors who nodded but said nothing, making her way to the bow of the ship. She passed Rosso at his station beside one of the cannons, and he put up a hand to stop her.

"I need to talk to ya about Alex and Little Titch." His teeth flashed in the scant light.

"This ain't the time, Rosso." Anne pulled away.

"They've ne'er held a weapon, save for an eatin' knife."

Anne stopped in her tracks to stare incredulously at Rosso. "Are ye sure? Never mind, ye wouldna said so if you weren't. Blasted greenhorns! Where are they now?"

"Down in the armory, getting' more cannon balls."

"Good, can ye keep 'em with ye? I don' want ta be trippin' over them."

Rosso nodded, and Anne continued to the stern wondering why on earth neither Alexandra nor Little Titch had asked for weapons training before their first battle; it spoke against their ability to be a future officer. If a person couldn't admit their insufficiencies, they'd not be able to learn what they needed. Anne shook away the thoughts and focused on the scene before her.

The shadows stretched long across the deck. The sun was nearly down now. Across the water, she could faintly hear the shouts of the crew on the target ship. Obviously, they'd been seen. There was no way of knowing if they'd been identified as friend or foe. The sun was directly behind them, and they'd appear as nothing more than a dark shadow in front of the ball of light.

A deep satisfaction filled her, and she chuckled quietly—they'd know soon enough. Her own crew was silent as they closed the distance. This would be an easy boarding for them. The smaller sloop was far outgunned—not a single cannon port marred its smooth sides. Anne smiled thinking of her five cannons, six-pounders all.

"All's ready down here, Captain," Peg said when she reached him in the bow. Peg's job was to organize the boarding planks. Five grinning sailors stood in a line down the port side, each with a long board ready to bridge the gap between ships.

"Good work, man." Anne took one last look around at her eager crew. Now that the fight was in front of her, she felt full to bursting with energy, the blood singing in her veins at the coming battle. It was a pity she and Mort had to sit this one out, but it was essential that they use this first battle to assess the worthiness of their new crew. She jogged back to the wheel to join him.

"Ease her in, Henry!" Mort called.

Anne leaped up the six steps to the wheel deck. She briefly regretted her decision to watch from above, but then she reminded herself that there were too many unknowns in her new crew. Before she got to Nassau, she needed to know who the deadweights were so she could rid herself of them. Better to miss this easy fight and save herself for the bigger battles ahead—a captain shouldn't fight in every battle. She flicked her gaze over each man standing ready along the rail. They looked nervous but ready.

Anne's Revenge slipped alongside the smaller ship. Waves sloshed between the ships far below the white faces of its crew lining the starboard side. She lifted the copper speaking tube to her lips. "You're outmanned and outgunned. Prepare to be boarded and we'll spare your lives." She kept her voice low pitched to disguise it. Men always seemed to think a woman would be merciful, and for some reason that made them fight harder at first.

The red-faced man at the sloop's rudder nodded. Shading his eyes from the sun, he searched out her voice, but she knew he'd be unable to make out more than her back-lit silhouette. That was the main reason for attacking at sunset, to blind them. They might be able to read her ship's name from this distance, but her own face would remain hidden a little while longer.

The other captain barked an order to his men. Thumping noises came in response—swords and knives dropping to the deck of the smaller ship.

The boarding planks lifted into the air. Henry bellowed into the quiet, "Boards ready, Captain!"

A breeze brought the smell of sweat intermingling with salt water to Anne. She lifted her hand and dropped it down sharply, the signal Henry waited for. With hollow booms, the boarding planks crashed into place.

It was over in minutes, a bloodless victory. Mort abandoned Anne at the wheel to join Rosso, Henry, and Clive stationed along the railing with pistols cocked while the rest of Anne's crew ran sure-footed across the boarding planks. They disappeared into the sloop's holds, reappearing in a steady line moments later with their arms full of loot: bolts of cotton, fragrant bundles of tobacco, and dusty bags of flour. Anne noted the tall figure of Black Brian among them, staggering under a heavy bolt of dark blue calico. She suddenly remembered Calico Jack in his best shirt, dark blue sprigged cotton, with a wicked grin on his handsome face. She shook away the image and the ache it left her heart and focused on the cotton. It would sell for a good price in the Caicos or Nassau. The crew would get generous shares soon.

Leaning beside Mort, Cookie bellowed over the railing, "Don' forgit me flour, ya daft buggers!"

Before the sun had moved even a full half-hour, a sliver of it still hovering over the horizon, *Anne's Revenge* was sailing away into the growing darkness, her holds now full to bursting.

Mort bounded up the steps to the tiller. "That was bloody boring. N'owt even a little fight in 'em. I shoulda stayed in me bed."

Anne snorted, "Have you forgotten how many men we lost to fighting o'er the years? I'll take a bloodless one any day. 'Specially if I get Cookie's supplies so's he stops grumbling at me."

"What'dya think o' the men? Ye wanna git rid o' any?"

"Ye mean other than Lucky?" Anne inquired acerbically. Lucky always seemed to be arguing with someone, but the man was a good fighter for all that, so Mort hadn't yet decided if he needed to leave the quarrelsome man behind despite regular complaints about him. She waved a hand to forestall Mort replying. She looked over the crew busy stowing the bags before she answered his question properly. "No. I didn't see any hesitation in crossin'. You picked good. Little Titch and Alex need some weapons training though. They can't be powder monkeys forever."

"Aye, aye las... Cap'n."

She gave him a sidelong glance at the near-slip, then swung the wheel over hard. It was time to head to Mayaguana and then the Caicos Islands.

She didn't plan to stay overlong at either place, just long enough for the quartermaster to sell everything he could before they continued to Nassau and unloaded the balance of their cargo there. Everything except the rum in their hold—it had most likely come from one of the Watling breweries in the Caicos or Bahamas who were highly unlikely to repurchase their own product.

If only she was so certain of her own errand on Mayaguana. She didn't know what she'd find, whether she'd want to depart right away or even where they might sail after Nassau. She was eager to confront James Bonny after all these years.

Mort snickered beside her. "Yer doin' it agin, lass."

She snatched her fingers away from caressing the hilt of her sash knife. "Don't call me lass," Anne snarled.

Ignoring her ill temper, Mort said, "I know sumpin's on yer mind."

Her spine stiffened, and she felt the armor she'd built to deal with her Da's friends slip into place, "I'm filling the terms of the Articles of Agreement as captain. We've loot in the hold, and as soon as it's sold, the crew will get their shares." She peered into the distance then made a small adjustment to their heading. Far below her, she could feel a slight difference in the way *Anne's Revenge* moved in the water—it was sluggish. Not quite wallowing, but the bones of the ship were fighting against the water. The new cargo needed to be rebalanced if they were to keep their agility.

Mort snorted, ignoring her frosty words and folded his arms over his barrel chest. "I got eyes. I can see sumpin's preying on ye."

"My personal business is mine own." Anne snapped, then took a deep breath and more calmly added, "Cargo's off-kilter."

Mort grunted sourly and stumped away to deal with the rebalancing, leaving her to her uncomfortable thoughts. She had to tell him something soon. Not sharing her plans with him felt like a hot coal in the pit of her stomach, and she did not like the feeling—Mort wasn't just her first mate, he was her friend. He'd been her only friend for many years. She had no idea where her search for her child and her traitorous husband would take her and no idea yet exactly how much he or the rest of the crew would need to know. As soon as she learned what she could on Mayaguana, she'd tell him everything then. He deserved that much.

The burning in her stomach eased a bit with the decision, and she put the rest of her worries aside. It was a beautiful night on the ocean with no land in sight anywhere, and she meant to enjoy the peace it brought for as long as it lasted.

Buried Treasure

"Land ho!" Limey called down from the rigging, his voice shredding with the constant wind.

"What's that agin?" Peg called back. "Lend whore? What whore? Where?"

A couple of sailors polishing the railings nearby chortled.

Limey glared down at them. The sole Englishman on board, the others thought it hilarious to pretend to not understand his accent. "Ya knows full well what I said. Bloody ijits."

At the wheel, Anne suppressed her own chuckles as Peg and the sailors laughed harder. Shading her eyes against the sun's glare on the water, she followed Limey's pointing finger to the southeast. She grinned at the thickening dark line visible on the horizon, proof she hadn't lost any of her navigation skills. They were right on target. The Bahamas were dead ahead.

She spun the tiller to the east, aiming for a point beyond the island. The Caicos and Mayaguana were roughly two days sail beyond Nassau. Two days she'd have to listen to Mort and Clive complain about bypassing Nassau. Anne sighed at the prospect and re-examined her decision to tell Mort after her visit.

"Captain, permission to speak?" Alexandra called from the base of the short ladder leading to the wheel deck. It had been a few days since their first plundering, and the young woman had settled into a routine and showed signs of becoming a competent sailor. Even Mort said that, given a few more months, she'd not be completely useless; high praise for him. On the other hand, Alex's weapon training was not going so well. She was cack-handed, and being right-handed himself, Rosso hadn't yet hit on the best way to teach her.

"Granted."

The young woman climbed the rest of the way up the ladder.

"I'd like to volunteer to stay aboard ship." The young woman twisted her cap in her hands. Her short dark hair ruffled in the fresh sea breeze.

Anne made a minute course adjustment then gave the young woman a sidelong glance. "Trying to avoid being seen?"

Alexandra gaped at her.

"You think you're the only one afraid of being recognized, Alex? Most of the crew have outstanding warrants on their heads, me included." Anne laughed at the dumbfounded look on the young woman's face. "When you need to know, I'll tell you my decision. Off with you." The lass would learn soon enough that a new sailor was never allowed ashore until their sea legs were fully formed—she would be kept aboard ship for at least a month to hasten the process. It would be hard on Alexandra as the crew was still making her pay penance for hiding her gender, but that was the lass's problem.

Alexandra bobbed her head and scurried away, bare feet slapping the deck.

Mort came up and relieved Anne at the wheel. "Sumpin' I need knowing 'bout?"

Anne shook her head. "New sailor questions. No need to punish her curiosity. We were all there once." A sudden memory of her first sea voyage came to mind. Her father had disowned Anne for marrying without permission, and her simmering anger at him had pushed her into working long hours to master every aspect of ship life.

"You want I should start tacking ta Blackbeard's Well?" Mort's tone was excessively polite.

Anne glanced at the dark line of land on the horizon. "Yes, I'd rather stay out of sight."

She'd told Mort their destination, if not the full reason for it, and he was a tad annoyed with her, arguing they should stop at Nassau first to unload their calico at the least. Anne knew it might sell for less in the Caicos, which definitely wouldn't make the crew happy, but the rum barrels in their hold told her their stolen ship was well known in Nassau. There would be time enough after her errand to risk discovery, and now was as good a time as any to see how far the crew would follow unexplained orders.

So, for the first time, she'd claimed Captain's prerogative to deny a vote. Mort and Clive, the quartermaster, had been forced to acquiesce. Clive was irate they'd not be offloading everything at the nearest port but was mollified by hearing they'd berth at the Caicos and then Nassau on their way back. Mort was contented by the prospect of finding some men he was certain would join their crew in Caicos.

Their current destination was Mayaguana. One of Blackbeard's wells on the far side of the string of islands, it was closer to the Caicos than to the Bahamas and Nassau. She'd been there once after she'd met Calico Jack in '17. He had hidden a clay plaque with their baby's adopted surname there in '19. But she had no way to return after Calico's hanging, and she'd blocked the entire visit out of her mind for years.

Leaving Mort at the wheel to navigate around Nassau, Anne returned to her cabin. Sitting cross-legged on her tidy bunk, she pulled the framed miniature of her son from its niche by her pillow.

Jack had always known he had a sibling. She'd never once considered keeping it a secret from him, despite his grandfather's demands. She studied her son's face and wondered what features, if any, her first child shared with him. Jack's hair and eyes were dark, the shape of his face was Calico's, but he had her smile. She wished she knew if her firstborn were a lad or lass.

There'd always been something preventing her return—first the need to raise Jack while steering clear of her father's many plans to marry her off, and lastly, her father's illness. Now someone was threatening to expose her secret, putting her at risk of hanging and ruining Jack's future. Perhaps it would be harmful to her first child as well. Not a child though—the babe would be nearly twenty-three now.

Once she had the name she needed, she would find her grown child and warn them someone knew of their parentage. Hopefully, she'd retrieve her stolen sea-glass heart at some point along the way.

After that, she would hunt down her bastard ex-husband and kill him for threatening her children and for giving Calico up to the English so long ago. Her hand tightened on the haft of her dagger again. This time she left it there and kept on staring at the miniature of her son and wondering.

She pushed away the memories of her recent nightmares of finding Jack drowned along with his brother or sister. Salt water ran through his veins, just like it did hers; he'd never drown.

She needed a distraction from her thoughts. Tucking away the picture, she headed up to the weather deck to watch Alex, Little Titch, and Black Brian's sword lessons and maybe even join in. It would be good to swing a blade and share some of her skills.

A few days later, early in the morning, *Anne's Revenge* anchored within rowing distance of the small island Mayaguana, better known to most as Blackbeard's Well. Blackbeard had claimed it decades ago, mostly because of the fresh-water spring in the middle of the island. Since his death, no one had taken the island, though a few ships occasionally used the spring, despite the tales it was haunted by Blackbeard's ghost.

Leaving Mort to assuage the crew's fears of a haunting, Anne went ashore with only Rosso, armed with a shovel, to learn who had raised her firstborn.

She and Rosso trudged up the slight hill in silence, Anne's thoughts preoccupied with remembering everything Calico Jack had said about where he'd hidden the information.

She took a moment to get her bearings and locate where Rosso should dig. Starting from the freshwater spring burbling out of a rocky depression at the base of some woody scrub atop a small hill, she paced off the steps and scratched an x on the sandy ground with her boot heel.

Rosso jammed the shovel into the ground, splitting the x in two.

Shading her eyes, Anne looked away, staring across the sand to where the ocean lapped at the beach below her. Ripples of heat flickered at the edges of her vision. She'd almost forgotten how hot it was in this part of the world.

A short while later, Rosso leaned on the shovel, panting in the thick heat. As soon as he'd recovered his breath, he turned to her. "Cap'n, there's nothin' here."

Anne stared into the dark hole, absentmindedly licking her dry lips. It was exactly 10 paces east of the well just as Calico had said. She wiped her brow with the end of her sash, limp with sweat.

Rosso's shadow stretched across the dusty soil, making him look taller. The elongated shadow caught her attention, and she understood they were digging in the wrong spot. She had counted off the correct number of paces, but Calico Jack had been considerably taller than she, so his strides were longer.

"Bloody hell," she swore softly. She pointed to a spot three paces further along, "Try there."

Rosso shrugged and rammed the shovel into the dirt again. The ground was much looser in the new spot, and he shovelled quickly. Anne stepped upwind to avoid the flying grit. After three or four minutes, a hollow thunking sound came from the shovel hitting something hollow.

"I found somethin'!" Rosso scraped away the sandy dirt.

Anne rushed forward to peer into the second hole. "Pull it out!"

Rosso dropped to his belly on the ground. Reaching into the knee-deep hole, he hoisted up a wooden box, perhaps two feet long and a foot wide. "This what we came for? Pirate treasure?" His teeth flashed in his dark face when he grinned at her.

"No one ever buried treasure 'cept in tall tales." Anne said absentmindedly as she stared at the broken lock dangling from the rough chain holding the wooden box closed. The edges of the break were shiny, fresh cut. She thought of how easily Rosso had dug this second hole, as if the earth had been recently disturbed. "Someone's been here afore us."

"Huh." Rosso grunted and lifted his flask to take a long drink.

She crouched in front of the box and pulled the chain from the brackets with a dull clink. Showers of dirt cascaded down. She lifted the lid, feeling the sand grit in the hinges and preventing it from opening fully.

The box was empty. "Sonavabitch! It's gone." Tears pricked at her eyes. "Dammit!"

"I'm right sorry, Cap'n." Rosso stretched out a callused hand before he pulled it back.

Anne rose to her feet. "Me too."

The sand underfoot shifted and the box sitting on the ground tilted. A small noise came from inside.

Anne dropped to her knees and forced the lid fully open despite the blocked hinge. Among the shadows pooled in one of the corners lay a tiny black velvet bag.

Her hand shook slightly as she lifted the small bag. It fit into her palm easily. It was dust-free and not large enough to contain a plaster imprint of a baby's foot.

She turned the bag over and her eyes widened. Embroidered on the bag were the initials AC. Anne Cormac.

It was hers.

Someone had taken the plaster cast and left this in its place. She jerked the strings open and upended the tiny bag over her palm. A small piece of red sea-glass fell out, and Anne's heart stuttered.

It was her sea-glass heart. But only half of it. They'd broken one of her most prized possessions—her lover's heart.

The dark red glass heart was the rarest piece of sea-glass she'd ever seen. Mary had given it to her when they'd first become lovers. The heart had been marked by a long fracture that nearly split the rough heart into two with only a small section holding the pieces together. It had been whole the last time she'd seen it a few weeks earlier. Someone had finished breaking it apart and left half here.

She crumpled the flattened velvet bag in her fist. It crinkled.

There was something else inside. She dug into the bag and found a small piece of parchment.

> *AB's two treasures.*
> *One kept at home and one left behind.*
> *Safe, for now.*

She growled, deep in her throat.

The treasures must mean her children—someone was threatening them. This had to be the work of James Bonny, her traitorous husband. He'd had Calico hanged and put Mary in gaol to die, and now this.

"Stupid childish games, I will kill that bastard for breaking this." Her hand clenched on the sea-glass heart, the newly jagged edges scraping her palm. Sand sprayed out from under her feet as she began stomping back to the pinnace.

Wisely, Rosso trailed behind in silence, waiting for her temper to cool. Anne might be quick to murderous rage, but it was apparent to Anne that he knew, as did everyone, that it was equally quick to pass.

Secrets Coming to Light

Anne's anger slowly settled into a cold rage as they made their way through the sandy dunes and then along the beach to where they'd pulled the dinghy up onto the shore.

Rosso's bare feet left perfect footprints in the wet sand along the water's edge. He glanced sidelong at Anne. Anne grunted and rolled her shoulders to loosen them, which he apparently took as assent to speak.

"Cap'n. What'd they take? And who took it?"

"'Twas James Bonny. I use ta be married to the bastard, so he knows me real name and me Da's. No one else would have known where ta find this heart." She showed him the lump of dark red sea-glass and handed him the tiny parchment scrap.

He scanned it quickly and handed it back, saying, "This sea-glass came from your father's house?" His eyes narrowed when Anne nodded. "If ya don't mind me askin', what was the treasure he took?"

"Not gold, if that's what ye're wonderin'. 'Twas information on my first babe. Before I had Jack."

"I'm guessin' Jack and the other are the 'one kept at home and one left behind'?"

Anne nodded. "I think so. I left me firstborn here, and I was with child when Da ransomed me free." She thought a moment before continuing, "'Treasure' could mean this heart, I guess. I've called this my treasure too."

"No." Rosso shook his head in disagreement.

She gave him a confused look. "What do ye mean?"

"I don't know Bonny personal-like, but takin' this heart don't feel like a threat. Takin' a keepsake, that's a taunt or a child's game. 'Cept for the 'safe for now' part, of course."

Now that her initial flush of anger over the theft was passing, she could think straight again. Rosso was right. James Bonny wasn't clever enough to have snuck into her home and stolen her heart. Who else would know her real name and where her treasure had been buried? She mopped sweat from the nape of her neck with one end of her long sash as they walked on quietly.

"But if ya want ta know where James Bonny is, I might have an idea."

Anne stopped walking and turned to stare at him. "Bloody hell!" She punched him on the shoulder, hard. "Why've you been keeping this from me?"

"Didn't know ya wanted to know." Rosso shrugged and rubbed his shoulder. "Don't even know if it's the same man. But there's a James Bonny in New York City. I delivered a shipment of rum to him a couple years ago."

"That is good news! We'll head there and get rid of our rum so's Clive will stop pestering me, and we can stop along the way to see m' thieving husband." Anne grinned, then turned serious. "Keep this to yourself, eh? I don't like having all the crew know my business." She took a drink from her flask, relishing the rum burning down her parched throat. She handed the flask to Rosso to seal their pact.

He held it loosely and stared at it for a long moment, clearly uneasy. Touching the flask to his heart he said, "Your secret is safe with me." He handed the container back to her.

"Ye don't drink?" Her eyebrows went up.

"Not that." He snorted a tiny laugh. "T'wouldn't be right."

The penny dropped. He meant a black man shouldn't be drinking from a white woman's flask.

"Ye know I ain't like that."

"I know. But others are. Better ta be safe."

Anne nodded, realizing there was some history behind this. More than what Rosso was saying, but she didn't push him on it. A man was entitled to his own secrets. As long as they didn't come back to bite her in the arse, he could keep them.

They reached the small dinghy pulled high on the beach. Rosso tossed the shovel in, then they each grabbed a gunwale and dragged the small vessel across the sand to the water.

It wasn't until they were well underway to the ship that Rosso spoke again. "Ya shared some o' your secrets with me. 'Tis only right that ya should know somewhat about me." He bent his head to the oars.

Anne waited.

"Ma and Pa were slaves. They died in '07 gettin' me and m'sisters out from the plantation where we was born. I don't know where their parents were from—Africa, I guess—but Ma didn't know, and Pa wouldn't say. Ma sisters live in Upper Canada, safest place for 'em right now." He took a deep breath. "I gots a price on ma head. I went back a few times to get others out and they know ma face."

"Ye fit in with us then. I escaped tha noose once too. I don't think I will again. Mort and a few o' tha others too."

"I knows that. I just thought ya oughta know why I'm wanted. I... there's more."

"There's never just one reason ta hang a man or a woman." Anne shaded her eyes from the sun glaring off the water and peered ahead at the ship as they drew nearer, giving him time to find the right words.

"Last time I went out to get ma cousins from the bastard who owned 'em, there was a little... scuffle. I didn't mean ta, but a wee fire broke out."

"How wee?"

"I believe it took most of the big house with it." He gave her a wry grin.

Anne grinned back at him, "Ye did better than me. I tried ta burn me Da's house when he wouldna let me marry James Bonny. Barely scorched tha main house, but tha porch had ta be rebuilt. I was sore disappointed... in my lack o' fire-starting ability at tha time as well as ma choice o' husband later."

Rosso was startled into laughing out loud and flashed her a quick smile.

Anne grinned back. "I told ye ye'd fit right in with us. Birds of a feather and all that."

He laughed again. "I reckon so."

He looked relaxed now, relieved to be rid of his secret. Anne knew that feeling well—she'd been forced to keep her firstborn a secret for far too long. It was a strangely freeing sensation to have someone else know about the child she'd left behind.

"If ya approve, I'd like ta sign those papers when we gets back to the *Revenge*."

Anne grinned. "Glad ta hear ye'll be staying with us. I'd hate if ye didna receive yer shares when ye'd been injured fighting for me." She nodded to the fresh scar on his forearm. She wasn't sure why he'd suddenly decided to fully trust her, but the feeling was mutual.

"'Tis just a scratch." He rubbed at the small wound and smiled back at Anne.

They settled into a companionable silence for the rest of the short trip back to *Anne's Revenge*.

It was a full week before they returned to the Americas. Anne's rage over the theft had turned to a slow burning fire inside—it was quiet and calculating and prone to small flareups, but after she knifed Seamus for arguing with an order, the rest of the crew learned to walk softly around her. Seamus treated the livid slash across his cheek as a badge of honour, but no one else wanted the same honour.

As soon as she and Rosso had returned to the ship from Mayaguana, she'd taken her first mate and quartermaster aside. While Rosso signed the code, the parchment that every sailor signed, making him a full member of the crew, she told Mort and Clive where they were headed after Nassau and why. Mort had merely grunted saying, "'Tis about time ye confided in me."

Clive's own good temper was fully restored by their quick stopovers in Caicos and then Nassau, where he lightened their load while the crew liquored up and made merry. Despite Anne's fears, no one seemed to recognize their ship, and they sailed away after three days without her having to set foot on the island where she'd spent so many hours carousing with Calico and Mary.

Fortunately, a good breeze filled their sails, and the return to Carolina took half the time of the outward journey. *Anne's Revenge* anchored offshore shortly after sunset, round a curve of land and out of sight of the sleeping Charles Towne, under strict orders to remain hidden until Anne and the others returned before dawn. She didn't want anyone in Charles Towne to know she wasn't secluded in her father's house. Men talked, and even the best of them couldn't be trusted to keep a secret when in their cups.

Sitting erect and tight-lipped, Anne stared straight ahead from her seat in the pinnace. Water lapped gently on the hull of the small vessel. In front of her, Mort, Rosso, and Paddy sat silently on their own seats as they slipped upriver. Behind her, two oarsmen grunted in unison as they rowed up Ashley River past the sleeping Charles Towne, heading to the Cormac home.

Leaving the oarsmen behind to guard the boat, Anne and the others crept through the underbrush along the river's edge until they reached the road that led to Anne's old home.

It was late enough that everyone was abed, and they easily evaded notice along the way. Anne's heart beat faster as they drew nearer, wondering what she'd find in her old rooms. She had the odd sensation that she was stealing up to a stranger's house. Despite having lived there for more than two decades, the large house had never been home. *Anne's Revenge* had become her home in a matter of mere hours.

Mort touched her arm when the house loomed in the distance, limned by the moon. "Movement o'er there." He pointed to the unused barn, a dark shadow behind the house.

Anne peered through the dark but could see nothing. "What'd ye think it is?"

"Men. Two, maybe t'ree. They crept 'round the side and disappeared inta tha ground 'tween tha house and barn." He shrugged.

"Not tha ground. They went into tha storm cellar." Anne's brow furrowed. It was near midnight, Sara and George should be abed. Perhaps they'd interrupted burglars, unlikely as it seemed. "We'll investigate this first. Go watchful."

Like wraiths, the four pirates made their way from shadow to shadow, aiming for the storm cellar door embedded in the grass. It was difficult to see in the dark, but Anne knew its location well, as she'd often found Jack hiding there to escape his chores.

"Ready?" she whispered. As soon as Mort and Rosso nodded, she opened the shutter on the dark lantern, flung the door wide and yelled inside, "Come on outta there!" She drew her cutlass, eager for a fight.

Unwelcome News

A confused babble of voices came from below, and Sara's face appeared in the lanterns glow at the bottom of the stairs. "Miz Anne? Is that you?" She shaded her eyes and peered up.

"What in hell's name are you doing, Sara?" Anne handed the lantern to Rosso and stomped down the steep stairs into the musty dimness. Behind her maid, she saw shining eyes, and Anne blinked, resolving those eyes into the dark faces of two men, slaves by the looks of their worn linen clothing. They were flanking a dark-skinned woman and baby huddled on the dirt floor beside a basket of bread. "What's this all about?"

The woman on the floor looked up, her arms tight around the baby. "I had ta leave," she said simply. "They sold ma chile and ma husband away."

Anne recognized the voice before she could make out the woman's face in the shadows. The woman was one of the slaves Anne had last seen at a neighbouring plantation, acting as serving maid for one of the ubiquitous parties of southern society. Anne pushed her blade back into her sash.

Sara touched Anne's arm, "I had to take Rosie in, Miz Anne. Everyone's in a ruckus with the news from New York. They say hundreds of slaves rose up. Everyone here's havin' a fit! They're sellin', beatin', or brandin' their slaves tryin' to weed out those they're callin' rabble-rousers. I just couldn't let Rosie lose her baby too."

"Shut the door, Paddy." Heedless of the dirt floor, Anne plunked down on her bottom and waved everyone to do the same. "Tell me everything."

As Anne kept asking questions and Sara or Rosie answered, the two men crouched beside Rosie gradually relaxed a fraction, their shoulders lowering every time they met Rosso's eyes. But Anne's own shoulders grew tighter and tighter in horror at the news they'd missed during their month at sea.

A small group of Black people had supposedly revolted in New York City in March and April. Dozens of free Black people living there had been slaughtered or deported from the city without benefit of trial. As the news travelled down the coast during the spring, panic had spread and a number of plantation owners near Charles Towne had hanged or sold off those slaves they deemed troublesome. Since then, every few weeks, another fear-fueled panic set in amongst the white landowners, and their slaves paid the price.

"She asked for help, Miz Anne. I had to take her in!" Sara finished.

The small group sat in silence for a long moment.

Anne worried over the story. She didn't entirely believe that anyone had revolted, or at least not in the way it was claimed. If those white men in New York were anything like her own father, they'd have jumped at the chance to slaughter free Black people at will. She looked at the eldest of the two black men, assuming he was their spokesman. "How many of you are there?" she asked.

Rosie nudged her elbow into the shoulder of the younger man, hovering protectively over her. He cleared his throat before speaking, "Just us. You know Rosie, that's Romeo, and I'm Capulet." The man who answered had a deep voice which rumbled straight through Anne. His accent reminded her of a French Jamaican pirate who'd sailed with her and Calico Jack.

"We cain't send 'em back," Rosso whispered hoarsely from behind her.

The old man, Romeo, flicked a quick glance between Rosso and Anne, obviously wondering about a Black man speaking so boldly to a white woman.

"I know, Rosso."

Romeo's eyebrows rose, and Capulet stifled a small gasp.

Ignoring their surprise, she mulled it over. Rosso was right, she couldn't turn them in. They'd be hanged or whipped at the very least. "Do ye have someplace to go? I kin take ye. I have a ship."

Romeo bobbed his head in reply and pulled Capulet nearer to him. He drew his finger in an odd pattern on the younger man's arm as if he were writing.

"Romeo says we go ta La Florida," Capulet translated.

Anne took a closer look at the old man. Romeo's dark eyes studied her in return. The dark skin of his neck was lumpy with scars. She knew he was the leader of this small group even if he couldn't speak.

Mort cleared his throat roughly. "I say we bring it ta vote." He meant to allow the entire crew to vote on changing their sail plan as they usually did.

Rosso's fists clenched, and Anne gave him a level look. "Yes?"

"Ya can't leave this ta the crew. Take the captain's prerogative."

"I'm not waiving prerogative on this, Rosso."

"Then I cain't sail with ya."

Her lips thinned with annoyance, "Ye'd leave me crew over people ye don't even know?"

"If I have ta. If none had stood up for me, I'd be right where they are."

She gave him a searching look before turning to Rosie and the men. "I've business in New York but we kin take you to La Florida directly afterward. It ain't out of our way. Mort, stay here and find out where we should leave 'em. Sara, get a packet of food ready. Rosso and Paddy, ye'll keep watch outside."

"She's good people. She won' give ya up in New York. I promise." Rosso said to Romeo. "I swear by all that's holy, she won' give ya up."

Romeo nodded shortly, but Capulet hesitated. He looked down to Rosie, sitting by his feet.

Without looking up from the baby cradled in her arms, Rosie nodded her own agreement.

Capulet glanced at Romeo again, then, visibly mustering up his courage, he looked Anne in the eye.

Anne gave him a steady look. "I know ye got no reason to trust white folk, but I won't betray yer trust."

After a long moment of meeting Anne's gaze, Capulet finally nodded.

Anne turned to leave. Sara jumped to her feet and followed Anne up the steep ladder. Rosso and Paddy trailed closely behind.

"Next time ye want somethin', Rosso, ask me. I don't take kindly ta bein' threatened," Anne said coldly when they reached the darkness of the yard.

"I didn't... aye, Cap'n. Thank ya for helpin'."

"I ain't doin' it for ye. I'm doing it for that woman and her baby. No woman should lose her child." Her own babies' faces flashed into her mind, and she banished the images. She didn't have the time to think on them; she had work to do.

Taking Sara by the arm, Anne slipped quietly across the lawn, still faintly annoyed at Rosso's lack of faith.

"Does George know about them?" Anne whispered before they reached the kitchen entry.

"No."

"Good. Ye keep yer ears open for anyone else lookin' for shelter but stay safe and don't let him find out." George was old and set in his ways—it was better to just leave him unaware of anything.

"Wait! Miz Anne, I have to tell you somethin'." Sara twisted her hands together. There was a strange note in Sara's voice, and it made Anne stop walking to peer at the younger woman on the shadowy porch.

Anne winced at the look of concern on Sara's face. She knew it must be bad news, but whatever it was, it would have to wait. "Not now. Pull together the supplies. I have to fetch somethin' first, and then I'll come find ye."

Sara nodded and disappeared into the pantry while Anne slipped through the darkened house to her bedroom.

The curtains were open, and thin moonlight streamed in, illuminating the room. Anne made her way to the dressing table and pulled a leather thong out from her loose shirt. A key dangled from it. She took a deep breath, then unlocked the drawer and drew it open.

A heavy object shifted inside, an oblong shape slipping to the front. She touched her pocket where one half of the sea-glass heart lay. The other half hopefully rested in this drawer along with her few pieces of semi-precious jewelry.

She wasn't sure why the thief had suggested they'd returned the broken heart to her. To discomfit her? Hurt her children in some way? Without knowing who the thief was, she didn't know why any of this was happening.

Her jewelry was still there in its usual jumble of mono-grammed bags. And right at the front where it was impossible to miss was a narrow wooden box that she didn't recognize. About the size of a small book, it was battered and worn at the corners.

"God damn it!" she muttered. She knew the strange box hadn't been there before she'd departed. It had been placed there while she was at sea, meaning someone had been in her private space. The idea made her belly clench with an emotion she didn't want to look at too closely.

She took a couple of deep breaths and opened the mysterious box.

A rough cotton cloth filled the box completely. When she pulled it out, underneath was a heavy flat piece of plaster the size of her palm. Even in the dim moonlight, Anne could see the shape of a tiny footprint pressed in the middle. The hairs on her bare forearms lifted. She caught her breath and reached into the box to lift the plaster out.

On the other side of the plaster, she could feel scratches etched deeply into the surface.

Moving to the window, she turned it over and angled it to catch the light. The roughly scratched letters read WATLING.

She whispered the name, her child's name, aloud. Another rush of emotion shivered over her skin, bringing heat in its wake. Ignoring the woman's flush, she ran through her next moves.

She knew where to go now. There were a number of Watlings in Nassau. They were the largest rum family in the Bahamas. One of them had taken her child in.

Someone knew who her child was and where that child—all grown up now—lived. Would they harm the child? Could learning their parentage harm them? How long was the memory of her actions in the old Pirates Republic? She couldn't think of any particular event while she'd been there that would warrant retribution on her child, but men's memories were strange. What seemed unimportant to her might be an unforgivable insult to another; she had crossed blades with more than one prickly islander during her time with the *Flying Gang.*

She gently ran her finger over the letters Calico Jack had etched into the plaster. Whoever had placed this box here in her room knew who she'd been in the past and where she currently lived. She had to find out who they were, how they'd tracked her down, and what they planned to do.

A horrible thought struck her. Perhaps it was her own firstborn child who was threatening to expose her. A shiver ran up her back at the idea. She had no idea what the Watlings had told the child about their parents. About her. She shoved the dreadful thought that her grown child might hate her aside while she carefully rewrapped the plaster, laid it in the box, and softly closed the lid.

Leaving the box on top of her dressing table, she rummaged through the drawer, looking for the other half of her glass heart. The small lined box wasn't there, and she tugged open the other jewelry bags rapidly and peered at their contents, then tossed them aside one after the other. Soon, she'd looked through all of them.

The other half of Mary's heart was gone.

Her jaw clenched, and it took a moment to master herself before she could think what to do next.

Pushing her jewelry bags to one side, she began to slide the box into the drawer.

The bags reminded her that she might need to bribe someone to get the information she sought. Anne rifled through the bags again and selected her most precious jewelry, a pair of sapphire earrings and a matching necklace, stuffing them into the hidden pocket behind her sash. Out of habit, she locked the drawer as always, despite knowing that the lock was now pointless. She smiled grimly at her ghostly visage in the mirror and went to find Sara in the kitchen.

Sara was there, filling a number of rough cloth bags with supplies. "You have more news? Give it to me straight," Anne said, bracing herself.

Sara took her at her word. She turned to face her mistress and spoke plainly. "Jack's missin'. Since early March."

Anne reeled. March. Her son had been missing for half a year. "What? How?"

"His commandin' officer sent you a letter, saying the ship went down and everyone drowned."

Anne felt sick to her stomach. Still distraught over her discoveries in her room, this new one knocked her back even further. She was horrified that she'd spent so much time looking for one of her children only to have the other disappear as soon as she took her eyes off him.

"Miz Anne. Here's the letter." Sara pulled it out from her apron pocket and offered it to Anne.

Numbly, Anne took it and stuffed it into her hidden pocket with the small jewelry bags. Jack couldn't be dead. Not her son. He just couldn't. And why had his superiors taken six months to advise her? Something didn't add up.

Sara laid a gentle hand on Anne's shoulder, but Anne shrugged it off. She didn't have time for sympathy.

"Let's go," she said gruffly. She snatched up two of the food sacks and hurried out of the kitchen, leaving Sara no choice but to pluck up the other supplies and follow.

Spoils of War

They had no horses to speed their journey back to *Anne's Revenge,* but they made good time nonetheless along the dusty road. Pistols at the ready, Rosso and Mort kept watch through the dark night while Romeo and Capulet hefted the bags of supplies over their shoulders. Rosie cuddled her sleeping tiny lass close to her chest, while she carried a whole wheel of pungent cheese liberated from Anne's kitchen slung across her back.

Anne kept her distance from the group. Except for Rosso, of course; she couldn't escape him. Since they'd unburied the ransacked chest a week earlier, he'd only left her side for his work training the youngsters in swordplay. Even then, he'd kept watch over her. From the glances he kept giving her now, it was obvious that he knew she'd been given bad news. The letter from Jack's commanding officer rustled in her hidden pocket. It was too dark to read it now—she would read it in private back aboard the *Revenge.* Anne examined her son's purported disappearance, looking at it from every angle. She did not believe for a moment that he had fallen overboard and drowned. That tale smelled as rancid as fish guts after a week in the sun.

A strange tension in the air pulled her attention back to the people walking with her. She honed in on it, leaving the question of her son's disappearance for the moment.

Rosie was at the heart of it. She walked a few paces ahead of Anne and Rosso, behind Romeo and Capulet who followed Mort. The young woman kept turning around to glance at Rosso where he walked beside Anne, not behind her as she undoubtedly expected he should. But Rosie said nothing, and Rosso was pretending he didn't notice her gaze. Those heated undercurrents swirled around to include Capulet and Romeo. Capulet whispered to Romeo, and, a minute later, the old man slowed until Rosie caught up with him. For a few paces Romeo walked close to the young woman and her child, their shoulders touching. Anne could see he was telling her something with his unique speech of writing on her arm. In the faint moonlight, Anne found it difficult to read Rosie's posture, and she couldn't see the other woman's expression at all, but Anne thought the young woman was arguing against whatever Romeo was communicating.

Rosso walked as if he were unaware of the others, his gaze flickering over the darkness beyond the road, but Anne knew him well enough to recognize the set of his shoulders. He was very aware of the slaves wondering about him and his relationship to Anne herself.

Having the escaped slaves onboard might cause problems, but even if Rosso hadn't suggested it, she wouldn't have felt right leaving them behind. She hoped the decision wouldn't bite her in the arse by giving her yet another conflict in her crew. She had enough to go on with Lucky's constant disagreements and the occasional fisticuffs. There was a good reason why the Articles of Agreement for life aboard ship was so detailed and why each man was expected to follow it—living in close quarters was a continual balancing act between strong-willed men all willing to draw swords at an insult. And women too, Anne admitted privately. She'd always had a temper. Seamus's new scar was recent proof.

The sky was greying into pre-dawn before they rejoined the pinnace hidden in the brush lining the river and the two oarsmen waiting there. The small vessel was crowded with three extra adults, but no one suggested making a second trip—they didn't have time before full sunrise.

The rowers worked as quietly as possible, and soon they arrived back at the hidden cove where *Anne's Revenge* loomed tall in the growing light. A rope ladder was dropped over the side as soon as they were recognized. Neither Romeo nor Rosie had ever climbed a rope ladder before, and Capulet whispered quick instructions to them.

As soon as the last crewman left the small pinnace, it was raised up. Amid the flurry of orders to set sail immediately, the three escaped slaves huddled together on the top deck. They refused to set foot below deck, and Anne didn't insist. She'd seen the overcrowded horror that was a slaver's ship.

Once the sails were set, Paddy retrieved blankets for Capulet to string hammocks on the upper deck near the foc'sle where the three newcomers would be out of the way of the daily work. The crew were used to living tight and walked carefully around the area. Hammocks were sacrosanct on board, being the only private space a sailor had.

Mort gave quiet orders to tack into the wind as soon as they'd cleared the cove and the shoreline began to draw farther away. Anne disappeared into her cabin to plan their route. If they didn't run into bad weather, it wouldn't take more than two or three days sailing northward to New York if they bypassed Charles Towne. Clive wouldn't be happy about that—they still had some rum and cloth in their hold that hadn't been sold during their Caicos stop.

Once alone in her cabin, she ignored her maps though in favour of curling up on her bunk and staring at the miniature of her son.

He could not be dead. She'd know it, she'd feel it in her bones like she'd known when Mary died, long before she'd received that particular missive.

She wanted to talk to the man who'd sent the letter, feel him out, and she'd see if his story tasted truer from his lips. She pulled the parchment out of her hidden pocket and stared at the name: Rear Admiral Thomas R. Harrington. He was stationed in New York, so she could kill two birds with one stone and talk to him before she confronted James Bonny while Clive sold the rum in their hold.

Taking a deep breath, she unfolded the letter.

> *My Dear Missus Cormac,*
> *It is with a heavy heart that I write to inform you of the disappearance of your son Lt. Jack William Cormac, presumed drowned along with his entire ship, in March of this year of our Lord 1741.*

It may help you in your grief to know that during Lieutenant Cormac's time aboard the HMS Alderborough, he behaved in an exemplary fashion in the performance of his duties and was due to be elevated in rank to Lieutenant-Commander upon his next landfall.

By way of thanking your family for your son's ultimate sacrifice, Lt. Cormac's pension will be deposited to your family's accounts before the end of the year.

On behalf of His Royal Majesty, I remain your most humble servant,

Thomas R. Harrington, Rear Admiral of the Red

Footsteps sounded in the narrow passageway outside her cabin. "Mort. Do ya know anything about a Rear Admiral Harrington?" Anne called out, setting the letter down on the bed beside her.

The footsteps paused then headed to her door. Paddy poked his curly head in. "I'm no Mort, but I knows the man. What do ye wanna ta know?"

"Well, for one thing, is he a truthful man?"

"Tha' depends on yer definition o' truth, Cap'n. 'Tis no secret he's up for Vice Admiralty of the Blue, so I t'ink there's no much tha man wouldna do ta better his chances."

"Thank ye, Paddy. That is very useful." Anne's thoughts raced through reasons why her son's purported drowning would be a chess piece for such a man, but until she met the man himself, there wasn't much she could plan.

From high above the deck came the call of a seagull: two quick squawks, then a third and fourth a heartbeat later. Anne grinned. It was the signal that they were coming up on a ship, a possible target. She carefully tucked the letter and her son's miniature into her desk drawer before dashing up top.

"Looks like a small merchant vessel," Henry said from where he stood behind the spoked wheel with Mort. He handed her the spyglass. "I don't think they've seen us."

"Douse the lights and run up the dark sails. I could do with a fight right about now."

Grinning, Henry waved at the cabin boy sitting below who came running to pass on the message.

In only a few minutes time, with barely a sound to carry, they were ready.

With all their dark sails hoisted, they skimmed across the water and were less than a hundred yards off from the merchantman when a faint call drifted across the water from the other vessel.

"Dark ship approaching at speed!"

They'd finally been noticed. Anne shook her head at the other ship's slow response time. She'd flog any man who let a dark ship approach this closely.

Anne shouted, "Ready, Arms Master?"

"Aye!" Rosso called back from his position below deck near the cannons.

The *Revenge* swung about, showing their broadside cannons to the ship ahead.

"Fire!"

A whistling six pound ball streaked through the air and smashed into the smaller vessel's main mast. Sails crumpled, and the other vessel visibly slowed.

"Bloody good shot, Rosso! That'll do 'em!" Anne scrambled down to the weather deck and hurried to the stern boarding plank.

"Take tha wheel, Henry," Mort barked and joined Anne, ready to board.

She gave him a tight grin while tying her hair back in a queue with a strip of leather.

The distance between the ships fast disappeared, and soon they could make out the white faces of the crew.

"Slow 'er down!" Henry called to the riggers. Wind bled from the sails, and they slowed.

"Boards down!"

One thump came, followed by three more as *Anne's Revenge* drew alongside the smaller vessel. Before the last stern board lowered, screaming men rushed over the first one.

The final board dropped in front of Anne, and she ran, sword in one hand and pistol in the other, screaming into the fray.

It was almost over by the time her foot touched the other vessel's deck, but a sweating man loomed in front of her waving a wickedly sharp blade. She slashed happily until he went down. Then came another man, and after him, a third.

A sharp whistle burst through the air, the merchantman's captain calling retreat.

Breathing heavily, Anne stared down at the bleeding men at her feet and wanted to howl. Whether in disappointment that there were no more or in triumph, even she wasn't certain.

"Ye could have saved me one," Mort growled in her ear. "I gets ta go ahead o' ye next time."

She laughed and clapped a hand to his shoulder. "Let's see what they've got in their hold."

"How's about ye get that arm wrapped up first? Ye're dripping." He handed her his sash, a long strip of faded blue cotton.

Surprised, Anne glanced down at her left arm. Blood dripped in a steady stream from her bicep. It began to sting.

"Thanks." She stuffed her sword into her own sash and wrapped the minor wound with the strip of cloth. "Let's get our loot."

Making her way to the hatch, Anne stepped over corpses and bloody puddles. A few of her men stood watch over the beaten sailors kneeling on the blood-spattered deck. It took a moment to locate the other captain slumped between the two hatches. His uniform was disheveled, and his hat was missing entirely, his bald pate glowing in the light of the nearby lanterns.

Unexpectedly, Capulet stood near the man, the sword in his hand dripped red onto the puddle by his bare feet.

"A good morning to ye, Captain." Anne said giving him a short bow.

His lips tightened as soon as he saw her, but he said nothing, glowering at her.

Behind her, Mort bellowed to the crew. A pattering of footsteps rushed down into the holds, and thumping noises soon came from below.

"Cap, go help t'others," Mort said. The young Black man nodded and ran.

Anne exchanged a look with Mort, wondering if they'd just gained another crewmember. Mort shrugged.

A straggling line of Anne's men began emerging from the hatch, arms full of their spoils: sacks and crates of everything from flour to lamp oil to cotton. They ran fleet-footed across the boards to *Anne's Revenge*, followed by a stream of muttered invective from the merchant's crew watching their cargo disappear.

The last of them ran across, and the boarding ramp teams began pulling the boards back. Bracketed by Mort and Rosso, with a grand flourish of her blade, Anne bowed again to the other Captain. "Thankee kindly for the goods. 'Twas a pleasure doing business with ye." She began to turn away but noticed a slight bunching at his waist under his jacket. She grinned at him, "I'll have yer money belt too, if ye please."

His face paled, but, at a flick of Rosso's blade near his chin, he reluctantly reached under his coat to unbuckle the leather strap of the belt. Flinging it at Rosso, he glared at Anne.

Rosso caught the flat leather scrip with his free hand. The contents jingled softly when he slung it over his shoulder.

Anne bounded across the single ramp still linking the ships together, heading back to her own vessel, and followed by the last of her men, all eager to see their new loot. There was nothing like the euphoria of battle to give one an appetite for loot.

Or for playing the two-backed hornpipe, she mused, watching Rosso's trim figure lope across the boards to hand Mort the money belt. He was a handsome man. Despite the grey strands in his tightly curled hair, he was well built and firmly muscled. Anne shook her head dispelling the unexpected lascivious thoughts. Breakfast first, loot second. Sex was a distant third.

"Henry! Take us awa'!" Mort bellowed into the morning.

Water slapping at her hull, the *Revenge* leaped forward underfoot, leaving the depleted merchantman behind.

Lucky's Bad Luck

On their second day of sailing north from Charles Towne on a heading that would take them to New York, Anne climbed aloft looking for a quiet spot.

Freshly off midnight watch, Alexandra was asleep in their shared quarters. The lass's snores kept distracting Anne from her work, so she abandoned her papers to perch amid the stern mast's rigging where she could think. She wrapped her legs around the gaff, stretching out the usual morning aches in her hips. It was time to ask Cookie to brew some more willow bark tea to ease the ache; she was nearly out.

She had a bigger problem to solve though: she had to find some other place for the lass to sleep. If Sara came on her next voyage, the two lasses could share a cabin and give Anne her privacy. Where such a space could be found on board was the bigger problem. Perhaps a section of the crew's quarters could be partitioned off for Alex. It definitely needed to be done whether or not Sara came aboard—a captain must have a private cabin. With the decision made, Anne turned her attention outward and surveyed her domain.

From her perch high in the rigging, she could see the hammocks of the three escaped slaves. As soon as the sloop had left their hidden spot south of Charles Towne, the three had scrambled back up to the bow of the weather deck where they kept to their small corner out of the way.

Capulet was the most sociable of the three, prowling the ship daily and asking questions of Rosso and the other sailors. He had a strong back, and by the end of the second day aboard, he was altering the jibs under the sail master's direction. Judging by his interest, Anne thought he might ask to join her crew soon. He would be a good addition.

They'd learned that Rosie was Romeo's niece and regularly acted as his interpreter. She didn't speak much on her own, spending most of her time with baby Cleo who was just beginning to walk. As one of the few women aboard ship, she was of great interest to the sailors. Anne told her to tell the crew to bugger off if they got too friendly, but so far, she'd not seen the young woman stand her ground, leaving it to Romeo's presence to protect her. The three were most comfortable with Rosso and the other Black sailors, with good reason. Many white folk barely saw them as human, much less as equals. It bothered Anne, but except for ensuring her own crew behaved better, there was little she could do about it.

Up above the stern deck, hidden by a billowing sheet of canvas, Anne swung her feet idly and turned her face to the sun, ignoring the chatter down below until a name caught her attention.

"That Rosie's some stuck up bitch, thinks she's better 'n me," Lucky was grumbling.

Anne sat up straighter and peered down. Lucky and Peg sat directly beneath her now, mending clothes in a patch of sunshine on the stern deck. Peg's bald head shone in the light.

Lucky looked about furtively before he continued, "Let's get her alone tonight. Split her beard, if'n ya know what I mean."

"Cap'n won' like that. Rosie ain't no wagtail."

"That jade'll never know. Don' know why Henry or Mort puts up wit' her airs. Thinks she's Cap'n just 'cause she sailed with Blackbeard and them lot."

Anne's jaw tightened, holding in a spurt of anger at the insult.

Peg put the net down, "Shut ya gob, ya unlicked cub! How many men you killed in battle? Cap'n's done for more'n ya kin count."

"Whiffle-waffle, she ain't doin' nothin' now. Where's the loot she done promised us? Mort'd make a better cap'n."

"Damn my eyes, if you ain't the stupidest man. Takes time to make a profit. And ya got yer share when we was in Caicos. Think she's gonna tell the likes of you and me what 'er plans are? Ijiit."

The grating noise of the nearby stern hatch opening interrupted them.

"Cap'n Anne?" Cookie popped his head out of the darkness. "Where you at?"

"Up here, Cookie," Anne called back, keeping her gaze locked on the men below as they looked up, Lucky going as white-faced as a ghost. "What can I do for you?"

"I gots your dinner ready, Cap'n."

"I'll be down directly. I've a little problem to deal with first." Anne swung down from the spar and thumped onto the deck a few feet from Peg and Lucky, hiding a wince at the flare of pain in her hips.

Peg leaped to his feet and bobbed his head, "I ain't with him."

"I know. Fetch me Clive and Mort."

His peg-leg didn't impede him at all as he hobbled off to the wheel deck at a quick pace. Anne stared at Lucky, sweating where he stood.

"I... I din' mean nothin' by it. Jus' words," Lucky stammered, the shirt he was mending forgotten by his feet.

"Tit for tat, Lucky. We live by our words, and we die by 'em too."

Mort, Clive, and Rosso came up behind her. "Captain Anne?" Clive asked, looking curiously between Anne and Lucky. As quartermaster, his was the job of ship discipline.

"Is Alex still the newest recruit?"

Clive nodded slowly, staring at Lucky who was visibly shaking now. "What's this fool done now?"

"He's planning to rape Rosie. Or mebbe lead a mutiny to make Mort the captain. I can't decide which annoys me more." Anne turned to Peg. "Do you agree as witness?"

Peg gave Lucky a grim look, "Aye, Cap'n. I so witnessed. The bloody ijiit."

Rosso winced and said, "I'll get Alex."

A thick silence fell while they waited for him to return. Lucky kept opening his mouth to speak, but only small squeaks came out.

Minutes later, Rosso returned with Alexandra in tow.

"Newest recruit has charge o' punishment," Clive said to the young woman. Turning to face Anne and the others, he proclaimed loudly, "Lucky here's been foun' guilty o' treason and plannin' ta meddle wit' a woman." He pointed to the box of sandbags. "Tie this weight to 'is legs 'n toss 'im overboard."

Lucky began sputtering and blubbering, "'Twas only words! I din't do it!"

Alexandra's eyes widened, and she shot a look at Anne.

Anne nodded at the lass. Crossing her arms over her chest, she leaned back against the railing.

Shaking visibly, Alexandra stepped toward Lucky.

"No! Don' drown me!"

Anne put up a hand, and Alexandra stopped in her tracks. "You want the throat?" Anyone found guilty had the option of choosing the manner of their death. Some chose to be left on a small island alone to live as they might. Others chose a more rapid death—slitting their throat.

"I want the island, Cap'n please, I don't wanna drown."

"You're daft if you think I'm willing ta go out of my way to find you a small island. Throat or weight."

Lucky gulped before whispering, "Island."

"Alex. You heard the man: he don't wanna drown. Get your knife out."

Alexandra pulled her knife from her sash and stepped up to Lucky, raising the blade in her shaking hand.

"Not here, you fool! I don't want my decks all bloody. Over there." Anne shook her head and pointed to a gap in the railing.

Grabbing Lucky's arm, Rosso dragged the crying man to the railing. "Face 'em out, with the wind at your back," he instructted Alexandra. "So's the blood goes out too."

Lucky began struggling in earnest, and Rosso made a quick jabbing motion with his head to Mort. The older man stepped up to the unlucky sailor's other side and snatched at his flailing arm.

"No! Ya can't! I want the island!"

"Good God, take it like a man!" Clive snapped, "Ye breaks the Code, ye pays the price."

Lucky twisted violently from side to side, almost dislodging Rosso, wailing the whole time.

Anne stepped up behind Lucky and grabbed a fistful of greasy hair bound up in an untidy queue. From this close, she could see droplets of blood trickle down from the tiny punctures Rosso's nails made digging into Lucky's bicep. "Stop caterwauling, you fool. Have some dignity," Anne snapped at him, then pulled his head back, exposing his neck. Lucky choked and gave a thick squawk.

"Can't I just make him walk the plank?" Alexandra whispered to Rosso.

Anne snorted. "We don't do that. Now get to work, ma dinner's waiting."

"Aye, aye, Captain." White-faced, Alexandra stepped in front of Rosso. She made the sign of the cross so quickly Anne wasn't sure if she had seen it at all, then Alexandra pulled her knife across Lucky's throat in a quick sweep. Blood jetted out in a sheet, sparkling in the sun.

Alexandra dropped the bloody knife and spun away with both hands clapped over her mouth, blood dripping down her arm from the sleeve she hadn't pulled away fast enough. She trembled and went a bit green about the gills, but didn't vomit.

Anne nodded approvingly at the lass. She let go of Lucky's queued hair and wiped her greasy hands on the back of his shirt, ignoring his twitching and the gurgling sounds. Rosso waited until the blood slowed, then he and Mort hefted the limp body through the gap and let it splash into the ocean. A few speckles of red dotted the railings and the deck.

Anne turned and saw the full crew had appeared on deck to silently witness the rough justice meted out. Turning to Alexandra but speaking loudly enough to be heard by all, she said, "I pay well, and I expect full loyalty for it. Ye plan mutiny against me, and ye're goin' overboard."

Eyes straight ahead, she walked toward her cabin beyond the watching sailors. A path melted into being at her approach, and the men ducked their heads as she strode past with her usual swagger, ignoring the pain that still burned in her hips from jumping down to the deck.

Rosie stepped out of the shadows near the ladder leading to the wheel deck. "Thank you," she said with quiet dignity.

Anne gave the woman a sharp look. She knew rumors travelled fast on a vessel, but it had only been a few minutes since Lucky had been talking out of turn. Perhaps this wasn't the first time Lucky had been at Rosie. She searched the Black woman's face before nodding. "He knew the price." Without the Code of the Coast, they would have no peace on board. It would be bloodshed all the time.

She'd had no choice but to put him overboard. The only question up to the captain was whether he'd be dead or alive when it happened.

She ducked into the short passageway, heading for her cabin and her dinner. She'd worked up an appetite.

A Question of Curiosity

"**I** canna keep the crew happy if ye don't let me unload cargo!" Clive thumped his three-fingered fist down on his desk for emphasis.

Standing in front of the desk, Anne snapped back, "We're no sailing back ta Charles Towne, ye fool! They knows me there. And they knows you and Mort. 'Sides we'll get better prices in New York for tha rum and cotton. And tha tobacco too." Anne rolled her eyes in exasperation.

Paddy stuck his head though Clive's door, interrupting their argument. "While we're there, add limes to your list o' Cookie's supplies. Little Titch and Jonny are weepin' from their wounds again." His curly head disappeared.

"What?" Clive's eyebrows rose, distracted by the news.

"They got scurvy!?" Anne shook her head in disgust. There was no reason to let scurvy get bad enough that your scars began opening up. A lemon or a lime a day was enough to ward it off. They must have been neglecting their limes since long before they'd signed up with Anne if they were weeping already.

"I know what scurvy is!" Clive scowled at her. "Those ijits got plenty o' limes to stop it, but they's too stupid to eat 'em," he snapped and plucked up a paper and waved it under Anne's nose. "I promised tha men their share when we sold in Charles Town! How's it look when we sailed past? Ye should ha' put it ta vote."

"Don' make promises ye can't keep. They'll still get their damned shares two days later than ye promised. In New York. When we sell tha rest o' tha cargo. 'Sides, they just got shares a week ago, in Caicos. These bastards ain't wantin' for anythin'!" Anne stomped out of his quarters and up to the wheel deck. She did feel slightly guilty that she'd gone against tradition of taking a vote on where they should next make landfall, although not actually guilty enough to allow the vote. Besides, they really would get much better prices in New York than in Charles Towne. Given time, Clive would see the sense.

Mort was at the wheel and gave her a wry smile when she joined him. "Clive still got his Irish up?" His tanned hands whitened as he twisted the wheel to hug them closer to the shoreline.

"Yup." Anne leaned on the railing beside him, basking in the sun.

"He's got a point, lass... Cap'n. We canna just keep sailin' with our hold full. Tha men want their shares."

"Jesus, Mary, and Joseph! They just got paid a week gone!" Anne glared at him, "Get yourself gone for a bit, leave me in peace."

"Aye, aye." Mort gave her a sidelong glance but left her alone.

The wheel was warm under her hands. She breathed as hard as if she'd been running. The noises her crew made as they went about the business of keeping the vessel shipshape were far away, muted. The motion of the ship—*her ship*—moving across the slow ocean swells gradually calmed her ire. She could put up with anything if she could keep doing this.

Sometime later, a small scuffle on the weather deck below pulled her attention off the horizon. Rosie and her baby huddled near the stern hatch, the patchy bearded Denny looming over them both. A grim-faced Capulet on the far side of the deck stepped forward, but before he could reach Rosie, Alexandra pushed in front of Denny. Using both hands she shoved the sailor back.

They were just out of Anne's earshot, but from the red ears peeking out from under Denny's hat, Anne knew he was getting an earful from Alexandra. His shoulders hunched close to his ears, and he shot a quick look over his shoulder at the wheel where Anne stood. She stared back, her face expressionless.

After another flurry of quiet words from Alexandra, Denny scurried away. Rosie touched Alexandra's arm and said something. Alexandra nodded and waved Capulet to come over. She said something to Capulet and Rosie who both nodded.

Before Alexandra strode away, she too looked up at Anne. This time Anne nodded. Whatever was going on with Denny, it looked like Alexandra had a grasp of it.

She waved the lass to join her on the wheel deck, a rare privilege. Alexandra's face brightened into a grin. She bounded across the deck, her bare feet quiet on the wood, and up to the wheel deck where she joined Anne. There was a long moment of silence between them. The sails creaked as the wind shifted slightly.

"I assume Denny won't be bothering Rosie no more."

"No ma'am... I mean yes ma'am. I mean Captain." Alexandra's cheeks turned pink with embarrassment.

Anne stared out to the horizon and pretended she hadn't noticed the young woman's slip. "Has that been going on long?"

"Since Rosie came aboard." She snorted a mirthless laugh, "The idiot didn't learn nothin' when Lucky got himself killed for goin' after her."

"Well then, that's interesting. Why'n't you come talk to me or Mort?"

"Mort said Rosie could handle herself." She paused before adding, "He said I shouldn't bother you neither. Not about that, nor anything else."

Anne rolled her eyes. "He thinks he's protecting me. Was there something else you wanted to talk to me about?"

There was a much longer pause before Alexandra blurted out, "I'd like to know how you went to sea. How you met... Calico Jack."

"Ah." Anne's lips twitched into a smile. "You wanna hear stories. Tonight, after dinner, I'll tell you a few. And if you want a little one to whet your whistle, I remember Calico hated fish. Didn't mind lobster or shellfish, but that man could not abide the taste of cod! Strange thing for a pirate to take a dislike to." She shook her head in disbelief.

Alexandra ducked her head to hide her wide grin. "I don't much like fish either. I only eat it when there's nothing else."

Anne laughed.

Popping out of the bow hatch, Rosso looked around, his gaze coming to rest on Anne and Alexandra at the wheel. He loped toward them, a pair of dull practice swords in his hands.

Anne nodded to the girl and pointed with her chin to the weather deck below. "Rosso's looking for you. After dinner then, I'll tell you how it came to be that I met Calico, and you can tell me why you ran away from home."

Alexandra's smile faded.

Anne scoffed. "Bloody hell, lass! You'd think I offered to cut your hand off. If you can't bear to share your story, how do you expect others to share theirs with you?"

"It's not that. My story is... boring. I want to hear what it was like being a pirate back then."

"Tonight. Right now, I believe Rosso wants to give you and couple o' others a lesson in swordplay."

That brought the lass's smile back. Her happy face sparked a quick flash of memory for Anne. Jack had had an equally brilliant smile when he'd been told he was getting something special. Ah, she missed her boy! It had been a long time since she'd seen him last. He couldn't be dead. Anne shook her head and refocused on the lass in front of her.

"You're cack-handed, so it's going to take some time to find a way of slashing that works for you. Do your best."

"I'll work hard, Captain. I promise." She ran off to join Rosso, who was now in a small circle of the youngest crew-members.

A wash of heat flooded over Anne, prickling her skin into goosebumps and making her sweat. She waited out the woman's flush while watching Rosso, Alex, and the two cabin boys, Black Brian and Little Titch, at their lesson. When the flush faded, she dried her damp palms on her trousers. A lump in one pocket scraped at her palm. The sea-glass heart. She hadn't put it down since she'd recovered it. "Paddy!"

Below her, in the officer's quarters, she heard him stirring, and moments later, he climbed up the stairs to her. "Cap'n?" He scratched at his rounded belly. Even weeks at sea hadn't yet trimmed him to fighting shape.

She handed him the broken sea-glass heart. "Can ye put this on a chain for me?"

He examined the small piece of glass dubiously. "'Tis only a bit o' glass like what washes ashore every day."

"I know. Do it anyway."

"Capulet says he's done some blacksmithin', and he's tryin' ta fix the block and tackle. Mebbe I kin get him to take a looksee." He bounced the small fragment of glass in his palm then strode away.

"See if he'd like to join us," Anne called after Paddy. "We could use a blacksmith onboard." If he had any facility at all, it would be a stroke of luck. Each man kept their own weapons sharp, and Cookie handled all his cooking knives, but even the simplest repairs to barrel staves, cannon mounts, or pots were beyond anyone's scope.

She raised her gaze to the horizon again. A few puffy clouds high in the sky and the huge expanse of rippled blue-green water soothed her. They would likely have smooth sailing to New York and the traitorous James Bonny, the bastard husband she'd left years earlier. Her jaw clenched so hard at the thought of him that her teeth ached.

If it were Bonny who'd broken into her home and stolen her Mary's heart, she'd make him pay for the brazen theft.

And she'd get information from Rear Admiral Thomas Harrington. No matter what it took, she'd find out the truth of her son's disappearance, even if she had to kidnap the man.

Tactics and Strategies

Anne and Mort walked at a brisk pace, heading for the most prominent building in New York's busy port neighbourhood: the British Royal Navy's headquarters. The pungent smells of fish, tar, and tobacco jostled for attention, but the salty ocean tang overwhelmed them all. It felt like home to Anne, although she hadn't been to New York for at least a decade.

The piers jutting out into the water were crowded with sailors, merchants, and a variety of unsavoury-looking sorts that made her wonder if any of them had ever considered piracy—she was still shy a few crew members. She nudged Mort and tipped her chin toward a particularly brawny fellow peacefully smoking a pipe while leaning against a bollard and watching a crew unload barrels from a vessel anchored nearby. Mort nodded, understanding her intent.

Looking down the length of the dock past the piers to the large building ahead, Anne tugged at her bodice, uncomfortable with the heavy cloth. She'd dressed for the part of grieving mother today. The shawl and feathered hat were welcome bulwarks against the chilly October wind, but her skirts and bodice felt decidedly strange and constraining after wearing a loose linen shirt and trousers for a month.

Mort was quiet beside her, his gaze busy scanning the men working nearby. She felt oddly naked without Rosso on her other side. But she couldn't risk him, nor any of the Black crew, on shore. Tensions were just too high in the city—more than thirty Black people had died in the recent riots, most of them hanged or torched without proper trial.

Rosso had smiled sadly when she'd told him he was to stay aboard. The way his brow was furrowed made it look as if he had knife scars all around his eyes. He looked downright disreputable, and she'd felt a startling urge to kiss those lines in apology. She'd covered it up with a gruffer than usual manner. "You make damned sure Rosie and the others stay below decks, eh?"

"Don't worry, Cap'n Anne, I know." Rosso had nodded. The three escaped slaves would hide in the *Revenge*'s cargo hold to evade notice. She'd seen the fear sweat on Romeo's forehead at the thought of being below deck. It was obvious he remembered his voyage into slavery far too well, but there was nothing else to be done if they were to stay safe.

She returned her attention to Mort, striding along beside her and grumbling under his breath as they mounted the three steps to the main entrance.

"I'll be glad when this is o'er," he said just loud enough for her to hear as they entered the well-kept brick building. He hadn't wanted to make the visit at all, saying that she was unlikely to get any more information than was in the rear admiral's letter. Anne hoped he was proven wrong.

Seeing a reception desk in the centre of the lobby, Mort made a beeline to the Lieutenant sitting there. Anne left him to ask after Harrington's office while she looked around the bustling entryway realizing that Jack had been here, perhaps many times. There were a number of uniformed officers in the large space, and the closest ones looked curiously at her.

"We're in luck, he's in t'day," Mort said, returning to Anne. He offered her his arm and led her to the stairs across the lobby.

On the second floor, Harrington's office was the third one down a wide hall lined with plain wooden desks guarding every door on one side. Long roughly-made benches adorned the other side, sitting below a row of windows that overlooked the street. The adjunct in front of Harrington's door took Anne's name and waved them to the hard bench before he disappearred into the office.

Anne sat quietly, gloved hands folded demurely in her lap, the very picture of a well-bred Southern lady.

The adjunct returned and held the door open. "Rear Admiral Harrington will see you now." He showed Anne into the office and indicated Mort should stay on the bench. Anne nodded to Mort and, mildly disgruntled, he sat back down to wait for her. She wasn't sure if he was annoyed by not being able to see himself proven right or not being near enough to protect her if warranted. She met his gaze and touched her sleeve where he knew her dagger was hidden and was rewarded with the ghost of a smile.

Harrington's office was plain, furnished with a simple desk and two chairs. The man himself came around the desk and offered Anne his hand. "Please, have a seat."

Anne sat in the offered chair, ignoring the twinge in her arm as the man's firm handshake had broken open the wound on her bicep. Offering a quick prayer that it didn't leak through the bandage still wrapping her arm, she studied the rear admiral as he returned to his own seat.

About sixty-five years of age, with a full head of greying hair and a neatly trimmed salt and pepper beard, he looked like every naval officer she'd ever seen.

"May I offer you refreshment, Missus Cormac?"

"No, thank you. I've come to ask you about my son, Jack Cormac. I understand he and his ship, the *Alderborough,* disappeared."

"I'm terribly sorry, but my letter outlined everything I know about your son's disappearance. I don't see the purpose of going over it again." He leaned back in his chair and steepled his fingers together across his neat coat.

Anne's lips tightened but she spoke mildly, "I've made inquiries, and no one has seen the *Alderborough* since November when she anchored in Savannah."

Harrington took a moment to reply, "We take these disappearances very seriously, we spent quite some time looking for it, hoping it would reappear, but it never did. Regrettably, these things happen sometimes."

"But it's been six months! Why did it take so long for you to contact me?" Anne pushed.

"There were 300 crewmen aboard the vessel. It takes time to write that many letters." His voice was cool.

"I've asked a number of other families whose sons were aboard and none of them have received letters," Anne exaggerated. She'd tracked down one family of a mate that Jack had mentioned to her but hadn't yet received a reply to her letter.

The colour rose in Harrington's face and his eyes narrowed. He leaned forward in his chair. "What do you wish from me? I don't know precisely what's happened to your son or the rest of his ship." His hands bunched into white-knuckled fists on his desk while his shoulders hunched closer to his ears.

Anne's eyes narrowed, cataloguing his reactions. He was lying; she was certain of it. He knew something about the *Alderborough*'s disappearance. His tiny surge of anger at her pushing proved it.

He did not seem like the sort of man she could manipulate through bullying or force. Time for feminine wiles.

"My son..." It wasn't difficult for Anne to begin crying. For years it had been her preferred tactic to manipulate her father as it was so quickly effective.

"Oh dear! Missus Cormac, please don't cry!" Harrington hurriedly scraped back his chair and came around his desk to lay a comforting hand on her shoulder. "We haven't stopped looking for your son. Don't lose hope."

Anne cried harder, hiding her face in her hands and hoping he'd keep talking.

"We'll find it, we'll get it back. I promise you, I won't stop until I find it... him."

She allowed her tears to dry up and babbled some grateful inanity to him. She had her answer. Jack was still alive. The Royal Navy wouldn't waste time on a lost ship. If Harrington was still searching, he wasn't convinced the ship had gone down.

He thought, or knew, that the HMS *Alderborough* had been stolen. He couldn't afford to admit he'd lost a ship if he wanted that promotion to Vice Admiral.

The only questions now were: who had taken the brigantine, and had they done something to her son?

She allowed Harrington to help her from the chair and lead her out of his office, wiping her eyes with the handkerchief she kept tucked into her other sleeve.

Her heart was soaring as she took Mort's arm with her head bowed, still playing the part of bereaved mother. She murmured some meaningless pleasantries to the rear admiral and his adjunct as they took their leave. Harrington reassured her again that he wouldn't stop searching.

As soon as they reached the street, escaping their gaze, she let go of Mort's arm and stood up straighter. "Well, that's that. Jack is alive."

Mort gave her a disbelieving look. "Ye were right? Th' admiral told ye so?"

"Not exactly. 'Twas his body language—I kin tell when a man's lyin' ta me."

"Well then, this once, I'm glad ta be wrong."

"A mother knows." She strode briskly down the street, kicking at her skirts which kept tangling against her legs in the stiff breeze off the river.

"Miz Cormac? I thought that was you!" a familiar voice spoke behind her.

Anne froze mid-stride and slowly turned to face the man behind her. "Master Slocam." It was the younger Slocam, fortunately. If it had been the elder, she might have regretted leaving her sword on the *Revenge.* The elder Mr. Slocam irritated her with his constant lecherous looks and comments, and now that she'd reacquainted herself with her weapons, the urge to slice into him was stronger than ever.

"This is a surprise! I didn't know you were in New York." Hal Slocam gave a curious glance to Mort beside her. Mort gave him an impassive glance in return.

"I have business here. And you?"

"Yes, my father's business takes him to all the major ports." His chest puffed out a little in familial pride.

"Is he here then?" Anne's hand itched to hold her blade. Her dagger was sharp but impractical for removing a man's head—if ever there were a man whose head needed removing, it was Harold Slocam.

"Oh no, Father is at home, of course." He couldn't quite meet her eyes and looked past her to the nearest vessel bobbing at the westernmost pier, a small freighter. "I'm here on your son's behalf."

"Jack? How did you... why did you..." She trailed off as she remembered that, as small boys, Hal and Jack had been thick as thieves until Slocam's father had separated them in a fit of pique over Anne's continuing unwomanly behaviour. Had the boys hidden their friendship behind Slocam's back?

Mort touched Anne's arm and cast his gaze toward the loitering stevedore she'd noticed earlier. Anne nodded her agreement, and Mort headed toward the burly man now chatting with two other men on the pier.

She turned back to give Hal a closer look. His shoulders were slightly hunched as if he were uncomfortable. His left hand fluttered at his side, a nervous tic she remembered seeing in the small Hal whenever he'd been caught in a misdeed.

"Your father doesn't know you remained friends, does he?" She hadn't known either. Jack was an expert at keeping secrets, a trait he shared with his grandfather and father. Anne herself could rarely keep a secret long. Her temper usually got the better of her.

Hal flushed, "No."

Anne chuckled and touched his arm, "Your secret is safe with me. I do wish I'd known earlier. I'd have helped you see each other out of school."

Hal shrugged, "Jack didn't want you to know. He…"

"He didn't trust me not to lose my temper with your father and let it slip." Anne winced. "He was not wrong."

"I'm not sorry you know now. I assume you're here to discover what's become of Jack?"

Anne nodded, the plumes in her hat bobbing. "I just spoke to Rear Admiral Harrington."

"Have you learned anything?" He looked eager until Anne shook her head.

Hal sighed, making it obvious to Anne that he knew how close-mouthed the Navy could be. "I've a connection to the admiral. I'm hopeful that something will shake loose," he continued.

Anne's lips tightened in annoyance. Hal was correct: it was likely he would get far more information than she would despite her position as Jack's mother. It was infuriating.

"I'll share whatever I learn with you, of course," Hal reassured her.

She briefly toyed with the idea of telling him that the admiral had let slip that a clandestine search was underway for the *Alderborough*. Perhaps she would in time, but not yet. She wasn't sure exactly how deep was his friendship with her son. "Thank you, Hal. I'll do the same if I learn anything. I'm away from home presently, but my maidservant will be able to forward any correspondence to me."

Anne waved to Mort to rejoin them, "I have urgent business that I must see to while I'm here, but I'm very glad to have run into you, Hal." She offered her hand.

"And I, you." He took her hand and eschewed the usual hand-kiss in favour of shaking it; as if she were a man, as if she were his equal. Obviously, he'd spent a good deal of time with her Jack. Her opinion of him ticked up a notch.

"A friend o' yer son, I take it?" Mort asked as they stood there watching Hal enter the Navy headquarters.

"Yes. He doesn't believe Jack's dead either." Anne grinned. "'Tis nice to be in company." They began the long walk up the dock to where their pinnace was tied.

"We gots two new men," Mort said. "They'll be aboard tonight."

"That's good news!" She might not have known where her son was at the moment, but she was certain he was not dead. With lighter steps, she strode back to her waiting *Revenge.* It was time to visit her traitorous husband, and she refused to be hobbled by women's apparel while dealing with him.

THE DEVIL YOU KNOW

As Anne emerged from the passageway leading to the officer's quarters, she found Mort leaning against a covered box of spare cords near the mainmast, waiting for her with a grumpy expression on his face. "This is a terrible idea. Ye need to take more'n one man ta protect ye." He glared down at her.

"I won't show him tha' I'm afraid." Anne gave him an even look. "One man is plenty. Ye can protect Bonny if I take the notion ta shoot him." She caressed the pistol's pearl handle, happy it was back in its accustomed place in the sash holding up her loose trousers. She felt more herself, more powerful, in this simple shirt and trousers than she'd ever felt in skirts.

Mort grunted. Assent or annoyance, Anne wasn't sure and didn't much care as long as he stopped arguing. She spun on her boot heel and strode to the gangway, Mort hard behind her.

The burliest of her crew were busy ferrying barrels of rum to the dock, and it took a moment for her and Mort to wend their way between them to shore.

"Where ta?" Mort said after they'd reached the main dock.

Anne stopped walking, letting the stevedores and sailors move around them. "Clive said 'twas the first street." Clive had been ashore just after sunrise to make his arrangements with various buyers and hunt down James Bonny while she'd visited Rear Admiral Harrington. He'd come back enthusiastic over a good sale and the precise location of her lily-livered husband, making Anne happy on two counts.

She'd met James after her sixteenth birthday and had married him within six months—something she'd bitterly regretted more than once. She'd been more in love with the idea of being married than in love with the actual man himself. After Da had disowned her for marrying without his permission, she'd convinced James to take ship to the pirate stronghold of Port Royal. By the time they'd arrived, though, she'd had enough of his whining and general spinelessness. Slinging a small sack of her meager belongings over her shoulder, she'd walked away from him, after only one month of married life.

The first smoky pub she'd entered had been filled with pirates ashore to spend their loot, Calico Jack and Blackbeard among them. With her long dagger at her side and her facility with using it, she fit into their number like a hand into a bespoke glove.

Anne shook the memories away. She hadn't seen James since that day, but everyone knew that he was one of the snitches behind the sudden surge of pirate hangings in '20. Calico and her entire crew had been caught and hanged. Of the *Flying Gang,* only she and Mary had escaped the noose, both of them being with child at the time; she with Calico's child and Mary with Mark's, her other lover. And now here she was, about to confront the bastard for the first time in more than twenty years. She felt energized by the thought.

She and Mort had to walk the entire length of the street before they found the weathered warehouse matching Clive's description. The blue paint on the door was scratched and salt-stained, with a faded sign reading "JB Trading Company."

"Stay close," Anne ordered Mort.

He sniffed as if to say she didn't have to teach him.

It was dim inside with long rows of piled merchandise looming out of the darkness.

"Kin I he'p ya?" A voice came from the shadows near the door and a hulking figure stepped into the light, his bald head gleaming.

"I'm lookin' for James Bonny," Anne said.

"Office." The big man pointed to a walled off corner of the large room. Light spilled out of the open door in a thin wedge that highlighted the dust on the floor.

Anne strode that way, her heels drumming on the wooden planks. Her pulse thrummed loudly in her ears in the cavernous space, and her fingers itched to hold her sword which she'd wisely left in her cabin. She'd dreamed of this moment for years, getting her revenge on her weasel husband for being the instrument of both her lovers' deaths. She paused outside the door to Bonny's office and took a deep breath.

She slammed the door open hard enough to embed the handle in the rough wall opposite.

The man behind the desk, elbow deep in a platter of oysters, mouth greasy, lurched to his feet. "Goddammit! What'dya think ye're playing at?" He glared at Anne and her companion.

She waited for recognition to dawn on him. It didn't take long.

His face blanched and the oyster in his hand dropped unheeded to the platter. "Jaysus, Mary, an' Joseph! I thought ye were ded!" He made a quick sign of the cross, touching head, heart, and shoulders.

"No' from lack o' tryin' on yer part." Anne noted his hair had gone grey and his eyes were now bracketed with fine lines. "I want what ye stole from me." Annoyingly, she noticed her brogue had deepened to match Bonny's—she didn't want to have anything in common with the man. She made a waving motion to Mort who sauntered around the desk to loom over Bonny as prearranged.

James dropped back into his chair and peered up at Mort before turning back to Anne. "Faith, woman, I'm a powerful man, but I canna bring th' dead back to life!"

"What? Not Calico, ye gibbering idiot! I want me glass heart. The one ye stole from me."

Genuine confusion spread across his face. "I have no idea what ye're on about."

She searched his eyes for duplicity. She'd once known this man very well. Either he'd learned how to lie more believably, or he was telling the truth. "Bloody hell in a handbasket. Ye really don't know, do ye?"

The bald man stuck his head in the door. "Ya need me boss?"

James shook his head and shooed the man away, then turned back to Anne. "I didn't even know ye'd escaped th' noose." He gave her a huge grin and plucked up a cloth from the desk to wipe his fingers. "I am right happy ye did. I didn't mean for ye ta be caught up in all tha'."

"Ye just meant for me lovers and me friends ta die?" Anne rolled her eyes.

"For god's sake, woman! Ye left me for anot'er man *and* a woman! What was I supposed ta do? Take it layin' down like a cuckold?"

Mort snickered, and James threw a glare over his shoulder at the other man.

"If ye'd been more of a man, I might not ha' left ye in tha first place." She caressed her pistol grip and watched James' eyes narrow at the movement. "Why didn't ye just grant me the divorce? I'd never ha' bothered ye again."

"I woulda if ye'd asked! You think I wanted to be married to ye? Ye tried to stab me!"

"It was only the once," she scoffed. "And I did ask! I sent ye a letter, ye damned fool."

James got a strange look on his face. "I never got a letter. But tha' explains Rogers' last words ta me before he hanged Calico. I think he stole yer letter before it ever reached me."

"Woodes Rogers had me letter? What tha hell for?"

"Ta keep us fighting? Who knows with tha' bastard? And if it makes any difference ta ye, I didn't give up Calico nor th' *Flying Gang*. I don't know who did, but t'wasn't me. 'Tis all water under the bridge, now tha' he's ded." James leaned back in his chair and looked her up and down. "Ye look as good as when you were first me bride. Th' years been good ta ye?"

"Fine enough. I'm lookin' for the man who wrote this note." She rummaged in her deep trouser pocket, pulled out the parchment she'd found at her father's funeral, and offered it to him.

James gave it a quick glance before returning it. "I told ye. I didn't know ye were alive. But now tha' I do know..." He gave her a considering look.

"Nah." Anne snorted, "As if I'd ever play tha hornpipe wit' ye agin."

"Ye wound me, woman! Ye don' know what I was gonna say!" James got to his feet and stepped around the far side of the desk, keeping distant from Mort. He stepped close enough to Anne that she could feel the heat from his body. Her hand slipped down to touch the hilt of her sash knife.

"I think I kin make a good guess. I don't care wha' a piece of paper says. I am no' yer wife." She refused to give ground to him, holding to her place in front of his desk.

"Ah! 'Tis a pity. I havena got a lady friend at tha moment, and I'm thinking 'tis time ta return ta ma lovely Irish lass." His eyes roamed her body, and his smile reminded her of when they'd first met.

She smelled the sweat on his skin mingling with the oil he used to slick his hair back. Although the lecherous look in his eyes was the same, this was not the same charming and callow youth she'd married. This was a man; he would not be as easily manipulated like the youth had been.

Mort cleared his throat, pulling their attention to him momentarily. He raised an inquiring eyebrow, asking if he should intervene. Anne shook her head slightly.

"I'd step back if ye value yer balls," she said to the man looming over her.

James looked down to see Anne's dagger hovering in front of his trousers. "Ye havena changed a bit, Annie! Ye're still me red-headed firecracker, even if th' red is fast disappearing." He grinned and stepped back a pace. "Canna blame a man for trying, can ye?"

He let the leer fall away in favour of a business-like demeanor. "If ye're no' here ta be me wife again, perhaps we can make some other arrangements. I assume ye've taken up yer old ways?" His eyebrows raised in question.

Anne exchanged a look with her first mate.

Mort shrugged. He didn't know what James was proposing either. Anne turned to James. "Wha' d'ya have in mind?"

"I've more requests for particular items than I can fill on me own. Would ye be interested in acquiring some o' tha more exotic items for a share in tha profit?"

"Could be. Is there something in particular ye want?"

"I have a whole list." James grinned and she remembered why she'd run away with him in the first place. He could talk a sailor into buying overpriced rum as easily as convincing a scared virgin into bedding him.

Not that she'd been scared then or now. If she were to stay at sea, she needed a secure place to sell any goods she acquired. An estranged husband might make a good, if unexpected, partner. It would be a challenge to outwit him, but she liked a little competition. It was good she hadn't succumbed to the urge to stab him and stuff him into one of his rum barrels.

She pushed him aside to walk around the desk and sit in his chair. Plucking up an oyster, she examined it, then used her dagger to pry it open.

"I see ye still got tha' dagger. Still as sharp as ever?"

She nodded, "Still looking for the blacksmith what did it. I could use a few more like it." She grinned at him and poured the oyster into her mouth. She watched the emotions chase across his face. There was annoyance that she'd taken his chair and an unwilling appreciation of her boldness, but the desire for profit won out over all.

James shrugged and turned to Mort. "How's yer handwriting? Not tha' I don't trust me wife, but 'tis always good to have yer agreements in writing."

Mort grinned and said, "She does like to wiggle out o' agreements when they don' suit her no more. I hear ye're cut from tha same cloth."

Anne snickered, and, after a moment, James laughed as well.

James rummaged in the cabinet behind him and produced a piece of paper that he handed to Mort. "Annie, get tha man a quill from tha drawer there." He slid the inkwell closer to the corner of the desk where Mort stood.

"Now then, I kin give you a list of th' items I'm looking for, but first we need ta agree 'pon terms. I give my other... suppliers... ten percent o' th' proceeds, seeing as how I'm th' one taking all th' risks selling th' merchandise."

"The going rate's more'n fifty percent ye cheating bastard!" Anne bounded out of the chair to stand nose-to-nose with James, enjoying the battle of wits. From the grin on James' face, she knew he was enjoying it as much as she. It was likely the only thing they'd ever truly had in common, their love of a good fight.

She settled into haggling terms she thought the rest of the crew would agree to, and that would make James wince, Mort chiming in occasionally. By the time she and Mort returned to

Anne's Revenge, the three of them had drafted a very profitable venture in various luxury goods ranging from silk and linens to silver jewelry and glass windowpanes.

A Crack Storm

While Anne was occupied with her husband, she'd asked Three-fingered Clive to make a few discreet inquiries about Jack's ship, the HMS *Alderborough*. As soon as she set foot aboard her own ship, she searched Clive out to find out what he'd learned. No one had seen the vessel since the previous autumn, months before she supposedly went missing at sea. It wasn't unusual to go such a long while without sighting a merchant vessel, but all Navy ships had regular ports of call, and the *Alderborough* had neglected two of these before she was listed as missing.

As they sailed away from New York, slouched in the chair bolted behind her desk, Anne kept mulling over the conundrum whenever she had a free moment but hadn't yet settled on an answer that made sense to her. The one thing she knew for certain was that Jack was not dead. He had not drowned. There was some other explanation for his disappearance and that of the *Alderborough*. She only had to figure out what, and then she could find her son. She'd be in Nassau soon to hunt down her other child and would ask questions there too.

With a brisk tail wind, they made good time down the coast to La Florida. Their current destination was just north of the tip of the peninsula where Romeo had informed them a number of Black people hid with a sizable native population.

"Storm's comin', Cap'n." Paddy stuck his curly grey head through Anne's door.

Anne looked up from the maps strewn across her large desk. "That so?" She peered out the windows at the molten sun in a clear blue sky. Beneath her feet, the ship tilted in a smooth rolling motion, sloshing the scant inch of rum in her glass.

"Peg's leg says 'tis a big'un."

"Well, if Peg says so, batten down the hatches and look for shelter." Anne said with no trace of sarcasm. Peg's missing leg hadn't been wrong in the six weeks they'd been at sea. Sighing at the need to delay sailing directly to Nassau, she mentally added two or three days to their journey to La Florida and began rolling up the maps. Paddy ducked back out.

A few minutes later, Anne followed him up top. Shading her eyes against the bright sun, she quickly scanned the horizon for the oncoming storm. Far to the southwest, an immense dark cloud loomed over the water, growing larger even as she watched.

"Damn my eyes! That *is* a big one. Tack away from shore, will ya?" she called up to Mort on the wheel deck. It was best to keep an autumn storm between a ship and the nearest land so as to stop a vessel being run aground in the massive waves. If they got far enough out to sea, they might be able to sail around the storm.

Mort snorted. "Whyn't ya teach your grandma ta suck eggs?" He didn't move the wheel, and Anne knew he'd already set a course farther from shore.

She bounded barefoot up the ladder to survey the ship's readiness. The two masts in front of her swarmed with men altering sails at Henry's bellowed directions.

If they couldn't skirt the storm while running south, most of the sails would be reefed or stowed when they turned to run northward with it, leaving only a little canvas up to power them through the storm. It was not safe to sail into a storm this time of year—October storms made for dangerously unpredictable winds.

Far to her right, the long black smudge of land on the horizon shrank and disappeared as they moved farther away. The towering storm to the south grew larger, a fat grey mushroom rushing toward them, darkening the sky and bringing up the waves.

"Looks a bad one," Mort said. His hands gripping the wheel were relaxed, though. He'd sailed through more than one hurricane—a simple storm would be easy in comparison.

She grunted agreement, estimating the size of the black cloud. "Think we can get far enough out?"

"Mebbe. We'll get some wet though."

Despite all the sails bellied out full into the wind, Anne had a clear view of the entire main deck. Directly below, Paddy barked out orders, sending crew to batten down the hatches and stow any equipment left out. Rosie and Romeo scurried below decks with the baby before the forward hatch was latched. As soon as they'd left New York, they'd scrambled back up to the weather deck where they kept to their small corner out of the way.

The last of the men aloft dropped to the deck from the rigging. Their work done for the moment, they went to their assigned stations and tied themselves to their posts. Even if one could swim, which was not a given even for a sailor, it was a death sentence to be swept overboard in wild seas.

Ahead of them to the right, the storm grew until it dimmed the sunlight into a grey twilight. Flickering sheets of lightning sparked in the towering dark clouds. The wind picked up, and the temperature dropped, making goosebumps lift on Anne's arms. Salty spray crashed against the ship.

Cookie appeared directly below the wheel deck, a large open crate in his arms. Seeing him, Paddy nodded. "Oil's ready!" he shouted over the rising wail of the wind. A dozen crewmen dashed to Cookie who'd put the crate down and was rubbing his back. From his crate, they each snatched a pair of dripping cloth bags bulging with oil. The bags were slung over the railing to bump along the side of the ship. The oil leaking from the porous cloth would deflect some of the waves from smashing over the main deck.

Henry joined Anne and Mort on the wheel deck. "We're ready, Captain Anne."

She nodded and looped an already wet line around her waist. Henry took over the wheel momentarily so Mort could tie a line around his thick torso.

The first few droplets splatted onto the deck, as loud as pistol shots.

"Brace left!" she called out. The deck tipped under her bare feet, "Here she comes!"

Mort spun the wheel, tacking them away from the rising wind.

A gust of wind blew sideways, drenching them. The electricity in the air energized Anne and tingled in her skin.

Rosso clambered up the ladder and joined them, ready to relieve Mort when he tired.

They skirted the bulk of the storm for the next hour. The wind bellied into the hung canvas, and Mort's weather sense kept him nimbly tacking port or starboard as needed to keep them square to the wind. Wind and rain lashed at them intermittently. The oil bags kept all but the largest waves off the deck. When Rosso took over the wheel, Mort ordered the riggers below to switch off before they grew tired and made costly mistakes.

At the beginning of the third hour, the unpredictable storm centre began swinging in their direction, and Mort snagged the wheel back from Rosso. Despite his quick work with the wheel, within minutes, the *Revenge* was enveloped in a warm driving rain. Anne's hair was plastered to her head in an instant.

"Damn!" Mort muttered, "I was sure we'd missed ta worst o' it." He wiped the water out of his eyes and squinted into the rain-soaked dimness.

"Furl the topsails!" Henry shouted over the booming of the waves against the wooden sides of the ship.

A handful of sailors, anonymous in the slanting rain, swarmed up the mast rigging, fore and aft. One of the figures slipped from the mainmast rigging and fell to the decking. Within seconds his replacement had scurried up the mast, leaving the injured sailor to limp to the hatch and tie himself down.

Silver Tongue Shelley started a rigging shanty, bellowing it loudly to be heard over the pounding rain. The crew standing on deck eased the lines, and the wet canvas of both upper sails slowly moved down to the spars where the riggers folded it neatly.

A slash of lighting lit the ship in the dimness of the storm, and thunder boomed immediately afterward, drowning out the shanty. The wind caught at the foremast's shortening sail, and Anne peered at it. Was one of the corners flapping? The forward line suddenly showed slack, and the sail's leading edge lifted.

The sail's lines were unbalanced.

"Halt lines!" Henry bellowed.

Too late.

The sail ripped free from the loose corner. It billowed full in the wind and knocked one of the riggers flying into the waves that crashed into the ship. Two others dangled from the rigging, unconscious or dead. The sail flapped free above the lower gaff, threatening the remaining riggers and putting strain on the mast itself.

"Cut sheets!" Anne and Henry shouted simultaneously.

The remaining riggers cut through two of the clew lines, and the sail pulled harder. Ducking under the flapping canvas, they scurried along the gaff to the rest of the lines. Squinting to see through the driving rain, Anne and the other officers watched anxiously.

A sharp crack sounded as the last lines were cut. The wet canvas lifted, trailing clew lines and bunters. The riggers clung to the lines below and ducked the wildly lashing ropes.

Anne sent up a prayer that the loose canvas didn't tangle into the other sails. The water-logged sail thudded heavily into the furled jib and boom but didn't snag on anything as it flew free. As it floated away in the strong wind, she tried to remember if one of the spare canvases below was a foremast topsail. If not, they'd have to cut one of the others to fit.

The ship tilted sharply underfoot as Mort tacked further away from the storm's centre.

"Jib down!" someone called from the boom.

Anne wiped her eyes clear of rain. The mast looked straight from where she stood, but that loud crack she'd heard worried her. Had it split? Henry now stood at the base of the foremast, peering up its length. Finally, he looked toward Anne and shook his head; there was damage. They would discover if it was only the top foremast or the larger lower one as well once they were out of the storm.

"Dammit," she muttered.

"Split?" Mort asked.

"Aye."

"Good thin' there's no canvas hangin' on it then."

Anne grunted. Capulet had certainly earned his keep when he'd fixed the broken block and tackle. Without it, they'd have a near-impossible task of replacing the lost topmast once they'd made landfall and could begin repairs.

Lightning struck, a blinding double flash that raised the hair on Anne's arms despite the rain slicking it down.

The last two riggers climbed slowly down to the weather deck. Anne peered at them. At least one of them was injured, but through the rain, she couldn't tell who it was.

With only one sail aloft, the mainmast's topsail, it was slow sailing to the edge of the storm. Mort's muscular arms vibrated under the strain of holding the rudder to their course against the waves pummeling the ship back and forth.

Another hour passed, Rosso relieving Mort and then being relieved by Paddy in turn. Finally, the storm began to outpace them, and the winds slackened. The darkness lifted as the storm moved away, the rain becoming slightly warmer.

Anne fumbled to untie her waist restraint, her hands cold on the wet cord. She then splashed barefoot to the foremast to assess the damage and find out which of the crew had gone overboard and how many others would be getting injury settlements.

An Offering to the Waves

Sunlight slanted across the weather deck, and a soft breeze washed across Anne's face, bringing with it the reek of pitch. Little Titch and Black Brian, the cabin boys, were using the sticky paste to waterproof the outside of the newest patch on the hull. Peg and Henry called instructions over the side to the boys. It had been a small hole, fortunately, and well above the waterline, a perfect teaching opportunity for the lads, not just for the repair but for the importance of properly stowing gear below decks—one of the spare cannon balls had flown free during the storm and smashed through the hull. It was only luck that had prevented further damage. Neither of the boys would forget to lock the chest again.

Behind her, where she still stood in the doorway leading to the officer's quarters, Clive cleared his throat, and Anne turned. She squinted to see him in the shadowy passageway.

"When did ye want to give Bert his send off?" he asked.

"Sundown, we'll have it then." It was the traditional time for a funeral meant to make offering to the waves in hopes of averting another disaster.

He bobbed his head in acknowledgment before easing past her and walking down the length of the ship, leaving her to her morose thoughts.

All over the ship, her crew scurried, fixing the storm damage. They'd been very lucky. Losing the upper foremast along with its sail and rigging had been the worst of it. The crow's nest was unsalvageable, but both nest and mast would be easily replaced once they'd made landfall.

It would be harder to replace Bert, the rigger who'd gone overboard with the sail. His loss made their crew short by four men now. Anne wasn't sure where they'd find that many. They'd already asked at every port they'd made and come up empty. She hoped Capulet would decide to stay.

"'Tis easy to impress a man, ye ken." Mort said from overhead where he stood at the wheel.

Anne craned her head up to look at him, not at all surprised he'd read her mind. "We ain't the Navy. We don't take men without a by-your-leave."

"True enough. But we needs tha men, eh?"

"No. I ain't gonna break the Code that far."

"Ye'd rather we were sunk by tha next storm?"

She glared at him but had to concede it was a valid point. "Bloody hell."

Taking her comment as assent, or perhaps permission, Mort continued, "Soon as we gets that mast fixed, we'll find a likely ship and offer freedom ta any man what looks the least happy ta be there."

Anne puffed out a breath, then shrugged. "As you like."

"Captain Anne?" Clive reappeared in the nearest hatch, both covers thrown back to help dry out the still damp hold where the crew slept. "Seems Bertie was partner to Frenchy. Kin he do some speechifying before ye?"

"Of course. Did Bert have much to pass on? I kin top that up with a half share if Frenchy needs." It was common practice among pirates who were long at sea to create matelotage relationships, a shipboard marriage. Anne had seen that Frenchy was devastated by Bert's loss. Now she knew the why, and her heart went out to him.

A scuffle from the bow caught her attention. It was blurry with distance but looked like a fistfight. Anne strode forward to deal with it, but brisk as she moved, Mort brushed past her and arrived first.

A handful of riggers circled around the combatants. Mort pushed them out of the way allowing Anne a clear view of the deck.

Alexandra knelt on Dickie's legs ploughing her fist into his middle. Mort grabbed the back of her shirt and lifted her in one swift pull. The circle of watchers suddenly found work to do, and they all melted away with the exception of Limey.

"What did I tell ye about fisticuffs?" Mort dragged Alexandra to her feet.

Unrepentant, Alexandra glared at Mort. "He deserved a drubbing!"

Limey nodded vehemently in agreement, "He was bad-mouthing Bert."

"There are other ways to deal with that." Anne gave Limey and Alexandra stern looks. "Unless ye want to be tossed overboard, get back ta work." A sudden flushing rose in Anne's cheeks, and she fanned herself.

"Aye, Captain!" The two hurried off.

Mort snorted. "How many chances ye gonna give tha lass?"

"As many as she needs. She's a good sailor."

"She's got an almighty temper. Back in m' day, tha' temper would ha' been beaten out o' her."

"In yer day? Away with ye, Grandad! Ye never beat no one for standing up for another. She ain't fightin' just for the sake of fightin' like some I know." Lucky had been the most contentious of the crew, and more than one person had remarked how much quieter it was with his absence.

"Reminds me o' someone. A red-headed lass I used ta know." Mort looked slyly at her.

Anne laughed. "That make you sorry for Alex?"

He gave her a twisted smile. "No, 'twas meant for a compliment."

Anne glanced at him. He began walking back to the wheel, and Anne joined him.

He cleared his throat roughly. "Wha's tha plan now?"

She gave him a puzzled glance.

Before she could answer, he continued, "I think ye should give up hunting for Jack and t'other. T'ain't right to put your needs ahead o' the crew."

"That ain't fair. We've taken three cargos in two months. I can do both." She thought a moment before saying, "If me plans bother ye so much, why ever didn't ye say so before now?" The question was very out of character for him. She couldn't remember any other time he'd asked about her personal affairs.

"Well... ye gots a temper, and I didna want ta be put overboard."

Anne snorted, "The sea woulda spit ye right back out."

Mort didn't laugh. "I bin hearing some grumbling about this goose hunt o' yours. Tha' maybe ye shouldna be Cap'n."

"Who's sayin' this? How are they hard done by? Didn't I just give out shares? Twice in a single month? And how the hell does anyone know what I'm doin'? Ye've been talkin'?"

"I'm jus tellin' ye what some are sayin'. And I didna say anythin'. Ye ken how rumors get turned inta fact from one person ta tha next."

"Until I'm voted out, we sail where and when I say. Get rid of the whiners next port." Anne snapped and strode off into the dark passageway below the wheel deck.

"Bloody hell, lass! I'm jus tryin' ta give ye fair warning o' a storm!" He called after her, his own anger matching hers.

"Don't call me lass!" Anne snapped, ignoring the rest of what he'd said. He'd get over his moment of anger quickly. Hers might take a little longer. Whoever the malcontents were, the best solution would be to get rid of them next time in port. Being short-crewed was preferable to bad feelings spreading throughout the rest of the ship.

She stomped into her quarters and poured two fingers of rum into her mug before plucking up the miniature of Jack from the niche where it now sat next to the plaster cast of her firstborn's footprint. "I'll find ye, me little lad," she promised and tossed back the rum. Within seconds, another woman's flush rose in her cheeks. Grumpily, Anne used a spare parchment to wave it away, wishing she could be in Nassau and New York simultaneously.

Henry stood on the weather deck directly in front of the passageway to the officer's quarters, riggers and cabin boys in a cluster before him, most of them yawning in the early morning sun. The quartermaster, Clive, had set short watches as soon as the storm was far off in the distance so everyone would have at least eight hours off watch before the heavy repair work began.

Henry called out half a dozen names. "You're on the upper foremast. Thank the good Lord that the main foremast didn't crack too. Get up there and tie it off with the block before you cut the lines holding it to the main so's we can lower it to the deck. We'll sail without it to the nearest island for a replacement.

"Alex and Little Titch, you'll pull out the spare main topsail. I'll show you how to cut it to fit the foremast once we've made landfall."

Clive stumped forward. "Ye canna use Little Titch for the stitching. His arm's all mashed."

Little Titch turned red. "I'm fine, Quartermaster!" He laid a raw-knuckled hand over the red-stained bandage wrapping his forearm as if to hide it.

"Yer not. If'n ye want yer wound payment, go sit yer arse down." Clive waited until Little Titch sat down before continuing. "Frenchie's done plenty o' stitching. He'll do ye."

Henry nodded. "Get to it." Nearly as one, the men leaped to their feet.

Anne held up a hand. "A moment. We need ta take a vote." Anne said to the crew before she turned to Henry. "I plotted our position. There's a few islands near but I think we should go ta Wassaw. It's not the closest but only adds a few extra hours. There's lot of timber ta choose a mast from, and we can top up the water barrels and maybe get some sassafras as the place is thick with it. What say ye?"

A leisurely day's sail south of Charles Towne, Wassaw was one of the unpopulated coastal barrier islands that protected the new colony of Georgia from ocean surges. It was also one of the least popular anchorages due to its small size, which was its best advantage as far as Anne was concerned, second only to its small crop of straight-trunked trees.

Henry glanced over the men, visibly counting heads to see if there were enough for a vote. "Who's in favour of going to Wassaw to make repairs?"

A forest of hands went up, nearly everyone in sight, and after a brief moment, Henry turned to Anne. "Motion passes, Captain."

"I'll tell Mort to change heading." Anne headed for the wheel deck.

Taking her departure as a signal, Alexandra and Frenchie headed for the hatch where the sails were stored, and the riggers began the climb up the foremast. There was plenty of work to do before they made landfall to look for an appropriate replacement for the upper mast.

Anne bounded up the steep ladder to the wheel deck. Mort was slumped over the wheel and she poked him. "Hey old man, no sleeping on the job, eh?"

He slipped to one side, slid down the wheel, and sprawled onto the deck.

"Cookie! Get yer arse up here!" Anne yelled over her shoulder as she bent over Mort and gently turned him onto his back.

Mort blinked slowly. The left side of his face slumped down as if it had melted.

Anne swallowed hard. She grasped it immediately—it was an apoplexy. It was a rare person who lasted longer than a week or two after one. One side of their body just stopped working.

"What's up, Cap'n?" Cookie peered over her shoulder, "Bloody hell."

Mort groaned quietly. The knowledge of his own impending death was clear in the single eye that looked up at Cookie and Anne. The ship around her faded away, and all Anne could see was her old friend staring up at her.

Gently, she wiped away a slick of drool as it dripped down his chin. All they could do now was make him comfortable for the time he had left.

Under the Black Flag

Rosso and Alexandra dragged the pinnace further up the beach. Anne wiggled her chilled feet in the hot sand, enjoying the warmth after wading through the cold water. Her hips ached dully from sitting on the hard bench in the pinnace.

She stood on a small sandy beach, perhaps 60 feet from side to side and defined by a roughly circular line of trees. Someone had built a large bonfire to one side of the open area, and a long row of barrels stood in the sand on the other side.

Nearby, grunting with effort, Paddy and Big Titch dragged a long piece of driftwood up to the fire, leaving behind a carved line in the sand. They lowered it into place behind a handful of other logs already there, neatly lined up.

She scuffed through the sand past the logs to the fire pit where two large kettles hung over the flames. The licorice smell of fresh sassafras tea came from one, and from the other steam wafted, bringing with it the scent of Cookie's stew. A wooden box with a large selection of pewter mugs and black jacks—leather tankards coated with pitch—sat ready beside the kettle. Two silver mugs sat in the sand in front of the box, Anne's personal mug and Mort's. Inside Anne's was a small bag of herbs. Anne sniffed it hopefully and was happy to discover it was Cookie's willow bark tea. She was feeling the ache in her hips today, and seeing the drawn look about Mort's eyes, she knew it was the same for him.

Putting the small bag in her pocket for later, she gave the two neat rows of logs and the crate of mugs a puzzled look. "How many are joining us?" she called out to Henry and Paddy who spoke quietly in the shade beneath the nearest tree.

"All of them, Captain." Henry called back. His freshly shaved face was creased into a smile, and he wore his nicest waistcoat.

She blinked and dug a finger into her ear theatrically.

Paddy chuckled. "'Tis time for bit o' levity, Cap'n."

Ah! The shoe dropped. The logs were seats for the jury and the audience. She grinned broadly. "Who's on trial this time?"

"Mortimer McCreary o' course!" Paddy shouted, slapping his thighs for emphasis, "He's the worst sailor, ye ken. N'er follows orders and 'e's now been charged with givin' information ta pirates. Perhaps ev'n bein' a pirate hi'self!"

Anne's eyebrows raised, and she turned to Mort who had been carried onto the beach and propped upright in a shady spot near the audience. His one good eye was looking over the parallel logs with a disgruntled look. "However did ye get talked inta bein' tha defendant?"

He rolled his eye at her and slurred, "I agreed if'n Annie Cormac was ma counsel."

She hid her reaction to his barely understandable speech and grinned at him. "I'd be honoured!" Scooping up the two silver mugs, she sauntered over to the stew pot and ladled both mugs full. Walking over to Mort, she dropped to the sand beside him. "We'll need some hearty sustenance for such a difficult task."

Mort grunted and twisted his head toward her. Anne pulled his personal spoon from his vest pocket, a beautifully carved piece of driftwood, and matter-of-factly fed him a mouthful.

"Don't be so down heartened!" Anne chided him, "Me Da was a lawyer, so I'm tha best lawyer here!" She chuckled at the lopsided sour look he gave her.

Henry called over, "Have you heard to whom he's accused of giving shipping records?"

Anne shook her head and shovelled a large spoonful of stew into her mouth. It was good, chunky with meat and potatoes.

Henry gave her a sly look, "Captain Mad Annie, of course, the notorious pirate!"

Anne choked, spraying meat and potatoes to the sand, narrowly missing Rosso's bare feet as he walked up to join them. He helpfully pounded her on the back. She waved him off and began to laugh at the absurdity of being both law-abiding counsel and piratical miscreant in the same trial. And that nickname! She'd always wanted a nickname, like Calico Jack and Blackbeard had. Mad Annie would do just fine.

She tried to feed Mort another spoonful, but he laboriously turned his head away. She gave him a troubled look but dropped the wooden spoon into his mug and nestled them into the sand at her feet.

Another pinnace pulled ashore, scraping across the sand. The two sailors in it leaped out and held the small vessel steady. A double handful of the men waiting splashed through the water to snatch up the lines attached to the pinnace. They laughed quietly among themselves as they towed the last of the empty water barrels ashore. The full barrels lined up on the beach were rolled to the water's edge and tied to the ropes floating behind the pinnace for its return to the ship anchored further out in the bay.

Anne watched them and ate her stew while composing an opening statement to defend Mort.

The sunlight streamed across the dry sand and flashed on the water. A proper chair was brought over for the judge's seat. Half a dozen men returned from the trees, rolling full barrels into the line awaiting transport.

Turning to look at the men who'd gradually begun congregating on the audience's logs across the sand, Anne saw Alexandra and Frenchie already at their assigned task of stitching the new seams on the freshly cut sail. Each had a palm thimble strapped to their hand to push the three-sided needle through the thick canvas.

Many of the men sitting there held a coil of cord or chunk of wood and a knife, fancywork to occupy their hands while watching the fun. Rosie and Romeo sat behind the others at the very back. Capulet sat with the sailor he'd become friendly with over the past week, Jim Draft, a quiet Black man who'd joined them in Nassau. Capulet looked very much at home with the crew now. She made a mental note to ask Henry and Mort to bring it to a vote to ask Capulet to join them. Asking an escaped slave to join the crew could be a tricky and dangerous thing and must be voted on, no matter how valuable he might be.

Two large smooth pieces of twisted driftwood had been set apart from the others for the jurors. From among the men crowding those logs, a grinning Peg waved to Anne as she surveyed the area.

The final tender ferrying men from the *Revenge* scraped up the beach—those left behind had drawn the short straw. Only the captain, first mate and quartermaster hadn't been in that drawing, of course.

Henry settled into the judge's chair a few feet away. The chair legs dug deep into the sand under his weight. Atop his head rested a wig that had seen better days, placed at a jaunty angle. The curls on one side had been flattened, and Anne wondered where he'd found it. "Court is in session." He waved at the log where Paddy sat as prosecutor.

Clearing his throat officiously, Paddy stood and puffed out his chest. A scattering of chuckles came from the audience. "Yer Worship, before ye sits a sorry dog. Lowest o' tha low. He sold his crewmates up tha river. His legacy is shameful, but he is still deserving o' tha mercy o' tha gallows, Yer Lordship." He nodded his curly head to the judge.

The judge nodded back, his wig sliding around. Henry reached up a hand to steady it. "I am the soul of mercy, sir. Carry on."

"No' only did this miscreant shirk his duties aboard His Majesty's ship, but he was in a position ta see cargo manifests and voyage plans, which he then shared with tha most notorious pirate Mad Annie."

Bursts of laughter broke out among the audience and jury. Anne suppressed a smile.

"How replies the accused? Are you ready to give your life for your crime?" Judge Henry asked Mort.

Mort cleared his throat, "Gots me a lawyer." He used his good arm to point to Anne, then pulled the useless left one down from its drawn position and held it across his lap.

Anne jumped up and began pacing back and forth in front of the sailors, sand kicking up beneath her bare feet. Some of the crew leaned forward in anticipation while others whispered to each other.

She gave them a stern look and waited until the whispering died away before speaking. "Yer Honour and gentlemen of the jury, before you sits a man wrongfully accused of dereliction of duty and of selling information ta tha dread pirate Mad Annie. I will prove this man innocent of all charges!"

"Hear! Hear!" a couple of the men in the back rows cried. Anne gave them another sharp look, and they subsided, blushing with embarrassment for the interruption.

"I contend that Mr. McCreary was, in fact, following orders by his own Captain, orders meant to misdirect His Majesty's men into believing tha' piracy continues, when all who know tha sea know tha truth—tha Age o' Pirates is over. Mr. McCreary's behaviour was not a dereliction of duty but rather a close adherence to it, proof of his unwavering loyalty to his Captain."

Anne risked a look at the jurors on their logs. Most of them gaped at her, unsure of where she was going with this defence, but a few here and there grinned broadly, enjoying the spectacle.

Mort snickered beside her; it sounded completely normal, unaffected by the apoplexy that dragged his mouth awry. His sash fluttered in a random breeze.

Shooting a quick look at the enraptured audience, Anne waited for Paddy's rebuttal.

Paddy stood up and turned to the nearest sailors behind him. "I needs tha Good Book."

Half a dozen hands near Paddy shot into the air, clutching tattered bibles. He plucked out the nearest one and stalked as best as he could on the shifting sand over to Mort.

"Ye gotta swear ta tell tha truth and nothin' but." He held out the book.

Mort laid his right hand gently on the cover, "I does."

"Are ye a pirate?" Paddy demanded.

"No!" He looked up at Anne.

"I object!" Anne called out, ignoring the quiet snickers from behind her.

"What? What in tarnation are ye objecting ta?" Paddy blinked.

"Ya can't just ask 'im right out like that!" Peg offered from the jury log.

"Hush, Peg, it's not your place to talk." Henry adjusted his wig again. "Missus Cormac, what are you objecting to?"

"The prosecutor canna ask my client any question that might incriminate himself."

"Objection overruled," Henry smacked a wooden mallet on the leg of his chair. It wasn't a gavel, but it did well enough at showing the gravity of the situation. "This man says he didn't do it. Does the prosecutor have anything else?"

Paddy scratched at his curly head. "Of course, Yer Honour! I believe this here man shouldna' be speakin' for himself. He ain't showing any o' tha good sense tha Lord ga'e him. He's even got himself a lady lawyer!"

There was a collective gasp and a number of uncertain chuckles from the audience and the jury. Anne hid her own grin.

Henry nodded and pursed his lips as he thought that over. "You have a point. Would you agree to the charges being changed to unfit for duty? On account that he's not in his right mind?"

"Aye, Yer Honour."

"Wait a minute!" Anne spluttered. "Ye canna change tha charges in tha middle of a trial!"

"I'm the judge." Henry stared haughtily down his long nose at Anne. "I can do as I like."

"Ye must obey tha law! Like any man must. Tha law is for all." Anne protested.

He sighed theatrically and rolled his eyes at Paddy. "This is what comes of letting a woman into court. I claim this man is *Hostis Humani Generis,* an Enemy of Mankind." He gave Mort a sneering look of mock disdain. "He looks the sort."

Paddy nodded vehemently in agreement, his grey curls bouncing, then winked at Anne.

"Yer Honour! That is uncalled for and against tha law! A judge must remain apart from tha prosecution or defendant. Ye've just proven that ye're in tha pocket o' tha prosecution and must be removed from tha case!" Anne said.

"How dare you!" Henry blustered, hammering his makeshift gavel on his chair.

"Mr. Murray! Ye must repudiate tha judge. 'Tis obvious he harbours disdain for both tha defendant and his legal counsel." Anne gave Paddy a stern look.

Paddy glared at Henry and shook his finger at him, "Ye ought ter be ashamed, Yer Honour. Ye're a learn'd man an' ye should be following tha law. As Mr. McCreary denies his guilt and there's na witnesses, I must drop all charges."

Cheers burst out of the assembled men. A handful even leaped to their feet and danced jubilantly in the sand.

"Mr. McCreary, ye're free to go," Paddy proclaimed grandly over the furor.

Henry tugged the wig from his head and peered at it for a long moment before he rose from the chair with a wry look for Anne. She knew exactly what that look meant: he'd seen court cases go exactly like this but always in the Crown's favour. They'd both lost more than one friend to judges who believed they were above and beyond the law.

"Court is adjourned," he said so quietly that Anne wasn't sure if anyone beyond her could hear him at all. Everyone had joined the dancers in the sand, and an impromptu jig had begun to the sounds of half a dozen voices raised in a victory song.

None of them could do anything about a judge making decisions that bettered only the judge's own position. Nor could they do anything while forced to watch a crewmate hang before them, but they could choose to live free—they could choose the life of a pirate where their voice counted.

Peg tossed her a bottle of rum. Catching it before it hit the sand, she took a long fiery slug before Henry snatched it out of her hand. Grinning, he took his own drink, then bent down and placed the bottle in Mort's good hand.

Anne grabbed Henry's calloused hand and pulled him into the wild dance. She swirled him around in the hot sand, whooping.

She would resume worrying about Mort and hunting for her son and her firstborn later, maybe tomorrow.

Today, they would dance and drink. Today, they would live free.

Paying the Ferryman

A loud thump reverberated through the timbers of the ship, shivering the golden liquid in Anne's mug and shaking the freshly dipped quill in her hand. She whipped her other hand under the tip to catch the indigo drip that threatened to blotch her note in the captains' log. Once the small emergency was dealt with, she remembered what the thump meant; the new upper foremast was being stepped today.

Not before time, she thought, leaping to her feet. She was tired of walking around the huge piece of lumber where it had lain on the deck for the past few days as it was finished. Yesterday, Henry had informed her that all the pieces were bolted in or tied on. The only thing left unattached was the new crow's nest, which would be lifted into place after the upper mast was lashed onto the lower.

Anne retrieved a thick, oversized coin from her desk drawer, hefting the solid golden weight in her hand. It would be tucked between the upper and lower masts underneath the thick layers of rope that tied them together. The coin was meant to pay their way across the River Styx if they were sunk. She wasn't sure if she entirely believed in it—she was educated, after all—

but the common sailors surely did, and keeping their minds at ease was worth the price of the gold.

She gulped down the last of the bumbo in her mug, the sugared rum burning pleasantly in her throat, and hurried to the weather deck.

A flurry of movement greeted her outside the officer's passageway. One hand shading her eyes from the bright sun, she gazed up the length of the ship to where Henry stood at the far end of the new upper mast that lay on the deck, talking to half a dozen sailors. Wanting a better view, Anne hurried up the steep steps to the wheel deck.

Mort was already there, leaning heavily on the railing overlooking the weather deck. Anne was surprised he was standing so well; perhaps he was getting better. Beside him, Rosso stood at the wheel—it was locked in position as they'd lowered all the sails to keep them as still as possible in the water.

Circling around Rosso, Anne walked over to stand beside Mort and looked across the weather deck. Two figures raced up the rigging of the main mast, dragging lines in their wakes. Another sailor, unrecognizable in the distance, kept pace with them from the rigging of the jib mast. They left a long line trailing between the two masts.

As soon as the three climbers reached the apex of the masts, one end of the new line was tied onto the brass hook at the top of the jib, and the other end was pulled through the mainmast's hook. As the slack was fed through, it would slowly raise another line, the halyard, which was draped ready across the deck.

Dangling from the middle of the second line was the block and tackle that would raise the upper mast itself. Two men kept watch so that nothing interfered with the block as it rose slowly, raising the halyard.

The hoist was already attached to the top of the new foremast. Distantly, Anne heard Henry calling out orders from his position near the top of the new mast that lay on the deck. Near the wheel deck where Rosso, Anne, and Mort watched, the bottom of the new mast was held steady by more than twenty men holding ropes looped tightly around it. Six of the strongest men of her crew stood midway between the two groups, their calloused hands gripping the other end of the halyard strung though the block, preparing to walk the deck and lift the new foremast into the air.

Well back from the mast, Silver Tongue began a crooning a halyard shanty. Anne winced at his choice but said nothing—the shanty man could choose his own song, even if it was one that glorified the English Navy.

> "Farewell an' adieu to you fair Spanish ladies,
> Farewell an' adieu to you ladies of Spain,
> For we've received orders for to sail for Pirate's Cove,
> An' hope very shortly to see you again."

Bursts of laughter drowned out the verse's last line. Shelley had altered the words from "Old England" to "Pirate's Cove." Anne grinned at Silver Tongue, who winked back at her. The whole crew lifted their voices in response as they pulled smoothly on the lines, and the tip of the upper mast lifted from the deck.

"We'll rant an' we'll roar, like true pirate sailors,
We'll rant an' we'll rave across the salt seas,
'Till we strike soundings in the Channel of Old England,
From Ushant to Scilly is thirty-four leagues."

The smell of raw wood blew into Anne's face from a brisk breeze, temporarily overpowering the ever-present scent of salt.

She held her breath as the tip of the mast rose higher with each response, the shanty man giving them a rest with each chorus.

"We hove our ship to, with the wind at sou'west, boys,
We hove our ship to, for to take soundings clear.
In fifty-five fathoms with a fine sandy bottom,
We filled our maintops'l, up the Sea did steer."

The men in front of the weather deck sang the refrain, their muscles bunching as they fought to hold the bottom steady as the tip neared its apex.

"The first land we made was a point called the Deadman,
Next Ramshead off Plymouth, Start, Portland, and Wight.
We sailed then by Beachie, by Fairlee and Dungeness,
Then bore straight away for the South Foreland Light."

Anne joined in the next response. The boards beneath her bare feet shivered as the men stamped in time to their words and their work. From the corner of her gaze, she noticed that Mort was looking drawn and shaky. His one-handed grip on the railing was white-knuckled now. His left arm was still drawn up to his chest, unusable. Every day, he seemed to get weaker, not stronger as she'd hoped. The coil of rope she frequently used as a chair when keeping Rosso or Mort company while on watch was directly behind him. She gently pushed Mort into sitting there and was dismayed when he sank down without protest. He blinked solemnly at her, his lip and eye drooping on his left side, then looked back to the activity on the main deck below.

> "We'll rant an' we'll roar, like true pirate sailors,
> We'll rant an' we'll rave across the salt seas,
> 'Till we strike soundings in the Channel of Old England,
> From Ushant to Scilly is thirty-four leagues."

"Have ya the ferryman's fee?" Rosso asked Anne as he tied off the wheel. With all the sails furled and being a good distance from land, there was no need to have a hand on the tiller.

She handed him the oversized coin, and he slid down the steep ladder to join the sweating men below, leaving Anne and Mort alone.

Rosso and a few others relieved the men working to keep the bottom of the mast steady. The foremast tip swung as it rose higher, and its base briefly grated against the smooth decking. Anne winced at the gouge that was left in the wood. Beside her from the coil of rope where he reclined, Mort's breathing was laboured. She kept flicking her gaze between the movement on the deck below and his ashen face.

"Now the signal was made for our fearsome ship to anchor,
We clewed up our tops'ls, stuck out tacks and sheets.
We stood by our stoppers, we brailed in our spankers,
And anchored ahead of the foolishest of fleets."

Everyone on the weather deck breathed in unison, all their attention focused on the same task; preventing the bottom of the heavy log from shifting uncontrollably. The men stamped their feet loudly as they walked the bottom of the new mast closer to the base of the lower foremast, lifting it with their overlapped ropes to prevent damage to the deck. The men pulling on the hoisting rope kept time with their movement so the bottom didn't swing wild. Finally, the men on the ropes circling the new upper mast reached the base of the lower mast; the mast was fully upright. The block line was released slightly, allowing the weight fully onto the butt end directly beside the mast it would soon top. Rosso and the others wiped sweat from their faces without letting go of their lines.

Above them, Anne could do nothing to help, save pray. Mort must have had the same idea—she saw him stretch a shaking hand up to touch the crucifix she knew rested under his shirt.

His breathing was painful to hear, and his colour seemed paler every time she looked at him. She wanted to get Cookie to take another look at him. The cook was the nearest thing they had to a doctor on board.

Anne's attention was drawn back to the mast as Silver Tongue sang the next chorus a little slower, giving them extra time to catch their breath and prepare for the next step—lifting the upper mast into place.

"Let every man here drink up his full bumper,
Let every man here drink up his full bowl,
And let us be jolly and drown melancholy,
Drink a health to each jovial an' true-hearted soul."

It took another repetition of the song to lift the mast up the length of the lower mast, going slowly and steadily.

Rosso ceremoniously passed the ferryman's coin to Henry to place between the upper and lower masts. Henry gave the signal, and Silver Tongue began singing a third repetition while the upper mast with its hidden coin was lashed into place. The lashing went swiftly, with half a dozen men tossing the rope to each other to encircle the masts. Tar was painted onto the thick rope in vicious blobs. Anne wrinkled her nose as the sharp smell drifted to the wheel deck.

She checked on Mort again and saw that he still looked pale and shaky.

"Would ye stop starin' at me? 'Tis makin' me nervous." His voice was slurred, and he swallowed some of the sounds, but his meaning was clear.

"You're looking a bit peaky there," Anne said.

"I'm fine."

Anne let his comment by. It was obvious to anyone with eyes that he was not fine. She turned her attention back to the activity on the weather deck.

Lifting the new crow's nest pieces went quickly, and large mallets hammered the pieces together with wooden dowels as large as Anne's arm. By the time the foremast was ready to hang sail, it was mid-afternoon.

Alexandra and Frenchie retrieved the sail while the last of the sheets were tied off fore and aft, and the rigging lines were extended up the mast.

Swarms of sailors climbed into position and began pulling the furled sail up into position. Anne watched avidly, remembering the first time she'd climbed into the rigging. A small part of her lamented that her increasingly stiff knees and hips kept her from the easy movement of the youngsters dashing nimbly in the rigging.

Behind her, Rosso cleared his throat. "Cap'n?"

She turned to look at him. Focused as she'd been, she hadn't heard him come up the ladder.

"Alex has a surprise for ya," he said.

"Is that so?"

"I tole her I'd let ya know ta watch."

Curious, Anne turned back to the weather deck in front of her. The sail was in position on the mainmast, and most the sailors were back on the deck, peering up. She searched for Alexandra, finally finding the lass exiting the forward hatch with a thick dark bundle under her arm.

The lass looked up at Anne on the wheel deck and grinned crookedly. She stuffed the bundle into her shirt and scurried up the rigging to the new crow's nest.

Anne squinted up at her. Only a few minutes passed before Alexandra began hauling something dark up the flagpole.

Halfway up the pole, a brisk breeze snapped the cloth out so it could be fully seen. A skull with two crossed bones beneath it—the Jolly Roger, the unofficial pirate flag.

Anne began to chuckle. "We're proper pirates now, me lads and lasses!" she bellowed, watching the black flag snapping in the brisk sea breeze.

Raucous cheers rose from every throat. "Cap'n Mad Annie and *Anne's Revenge!*"

Anne grinned over her shoulder at Rosso. "Did you have something to do with this?"

"'Twas Mort. A while back, he told the lass we had some black canvas going ta waste in storage."

She turned to Mort slouched in the rope coil. "Thank ye, man. It didn't feel entirely right sailing without one o' those."

He gave her a lopsided smile. "Easier ta ask favour if'n ye're pleased."

Anne frowned and exchanged a puzzled look with Rosso. He shrugged and pushed her gently away from the wheel so he could untie it. "Ye'll have to ask him."

Despite the pain in her hips, she crouched down in front of Mort. "What kind o' favour?"

"End ma misery."

Anne jerked back and fell onto her rump. Rosso leaned down to offer her a hand. "Did ye know about this?" she demanded of the weapons master, ignoring his hand and pulling herself upright with the railing.

"Yes."

She glared at Mort and then Rosso, then back to Mort again. "Why?"

"Dyin' hurts."

"Sweet Jesus, man! I cain't. You're ma friend."

"S'why I asked ye." Mort gave her a calm look.

Anne sighed. He was right, though—this was the kind of thing you could only ask a friend. A close friend. "Have ye got a preference?" she said at last.

Rosso cleared his throat. Anne and Mort turned to face him. "Across the arm is least painful. I'll help Cap'n Anne get you comfortable."

Mort nodded, "Firs' mate's duty."

Anne flicked a look at Mort—he'd obviously been thinking about who could replace him—then she nodded in agreement. Rosso was a good choice for first mate. Over the weeks they'd been sailing, she'd gotten to know him, as had the crew. He'd been proven trustworthy, and he was an admirable sailor and weapons expert.

Anne looked back at Mort's craggy face. "I'll miss ye, man," she said. She'd known him for more than three decades. His friendship had kept her sane during the early years of raising Jack and avoiding the suitors her father kept flinging at her.

Mort gave her a crooked grin, "Ye'll do fine wit'out me, lass."

"Don't call me lass," Anne scolded, the words tearing at her throat as she realized that this would likely be the last time he'd call her lass.

"Give Jack... ma best."

Anne nodded. "I will."

Rosso plucked up a well-used silver bleeding basin from behind the ropes and handed it to Anne. She hadn't noticed the basin on the wheel deck. Rosso must have brought it in anticipation. She frowned at him but accepted it. She shook her head to dispel the thought and sat down beside Mort. Gently, she reached across his body and lifted his contorted left arm and slid the basin into place under it. She didn't have a fleam, but her dagger would do. It seemed a fitting choice: a never-dull blade for the man who'd kept her sharp over the decades.

"Are ye sure, Mort?"

Holding her gaze, he nodded. "Paid the ferryman." His good arm pointed to the newly installed mast with its hidden coin.

Anne nodded and, while he was distracted, swiftly drew the familiar bloodletting line across his arm.

Mort smiled at her. The unnatural crookedness of the smile caught at her heart. He grasped her free hand and held it tightly. A steady dripping plinked into the tarnished basin. Slowly, Mort's eyes closed, and he drifted away.

Tears filled Anne's eyes and she let go of the basin to reach blindly across Mort for Rosso's hand. He took it silently, crouching by the wheel. She gripped it tightly, closing her own eyes and let her memories of their friendship unspool as Mort's hand grew cold in hers.

Land of Flowers

The air was close and hot in her cabin. Anne opened the mullioned stern window and propped her door ajar, allowing a small cross breeze, but sweat still trickled down her neck and between her breasts. She plucked the damp linen of her shirt away from her overheated skin and sighed, staring down at the maps on her desk.

Overhead, footsteps crossed the wheel deck, and farther away, one of the hatch covers slammed shut with a hollow boom that shivered through the beams of the ship.

She let the maps curl up on her desk, then sighed again and tossed them into the map box bolted to the floor before fleeing the stifling room.

Up on deck, the breeze was a little stronger, shifting here and there in brief spurts that flung Anne's hair into her eyes and out again. Between the unrelenting heat exaggerated by the damned women's flushes that kept plaguing her, the fickle wind, and intermittent stomach cramps, she felt grumpy and irritable. She climbed up to the wheel deck where Rosso manned the wheel for midday watch.

"Why don't I have a chair up here?" Anne groused as she crossed behind him to sprawl on the coil of rope, trying to banish the memory of Mort laying there.

"Bloody hell. That would look a sight, wouldn't it?" he said, snorting with laughter, a familiar little sound she occasionally found rather endearing. Except when he aimed it at her like now.

Anne grunted. She stared between the balusters of the railing out over the deck. She could see Capulet and Rosie sitting on the aft hatch, talking quietly while she nursed her baby.

A memory of nursing Jack swept over her, and her heart clenched at the idea that her children might be dead. She refused to even consider it.

Jack was a strong swimmer. It made no sense that he'd fallen overboard, nor could she believe he'd drowned. She could see no reason for the Admiral to have lied about this. Furthermore, why hadn't his ship been marked as 'lost at sea' until six months after its disappearance? None of Clive's sources had seen the HMS *Alderborough* since last autumn. Something strange was going on. She was certain of it.

"Cap'n Anne." Capulet called out softly.

She peered around Rosso's legs and the wheel. Capulet stood on the top step of the short ladder to the wheel deck. "Yes?"

Capulet clenched his hands tightly together. If he'd had a cap, Anne was sure he'd have been twisting it nervously. "Jim says you're lookin' for your boy."

"Yes, that's right. Jack Cormac." Her heart skipped a beat.

"I saw a feller in Nassau when Massa bought me, name of Cormac. Skinny lad couple years younger than me 'n taller wit' a Navy uniform."

Anne scrambled to her feet, suppressing a wince at the stiffness in her hips, and asked, "When was this?"

"Spring, Cap'n."

"What month?" she demanded, a sudden excitement filling her.

"Early April."

Six months ago. *After* Jack had supposedly drowned when his ship went down. Anne's heart leaped then crashed back down; perhaps it wasn't her Jack. How could she be sure? She remembered Jack's miniature. "Wait here." She brushed past him on the steps and hurried to her cabin. A few minutes later, she shoved the small miniature of Jack in front of Capulet's face. "This the fellow you saw?"

"Yes ma'am!" Capulet nodded, "That's him, sure 'nuff!"

Her heart felt near to bursting with happiness, but she kept it well hidden. "Then I was lied to. He didn't drown."

"I figured you should know, seeing as how you're helpin' us."

"I appreciate that, Capulet."

He ducked his head and returned to sit with Rosie.

"That's a lucky piece of news." Rosso said. He scanned the horizon. "Another reason ta head back ta Nassau."

"Don't need another reason." She barked a short laugh. "We've got a hold full of cargo that Clive is desperate to sell off." A few days after Mort's death, they'd run into a small vessel that had yielded a number of fine pieces of jewelry in addition to the more usual foodstuffs and dry goods. "I'd like to look for some of those specialty items Bonny wants." She leaned on the railing and turned to face him. "Just as soon as we drop off our friends in La Florida."

The muscles bunched under his rolled-up shirt sleeves as he swung the wheel. "I reckon the crew'd like a spell in their old haunts."

Anne nodded. There'd been quite a few grumbles about not getting shore leave since New York. Even hungover from days of drunken debauchery during leave, some men would grumble over wanting more. Being aground for ship repairs didn't count even if the sailors were off duty with little to do—there was no drinking or carousing to be had on a deserted island, and having two funerals and one memorial in a week had left the men eager for relief that didn't come from a bottle but from the company of women.

She grinned at Rosso. "You got an old haunt there? You didn't get any leave in New York nor when we had to fix the mast."

"Mebbe. I've been ta Nassau once or twice. Years back now so I doubt anyone recollects me." He kept his gaze on the horizon.

She gave him a searching look and prodded a little, "Sounds like you might'a left someone special there."

"If we run up the rest of the sails, we'll get there a mite quicker," Rosso said, avoiding her unspoken question.

"Good idea." She let him change the subject. She'd have plenty of time before arriving in Nassau to grill him properly.

"Full sail, Sailmaster!" Rosso bellowed over the railing.

"Aye!" Henry called back. Within minutes, every scrap of canvas was bellying up to the light wind, and *Anne's Revenge* was flying across the waves.

The sun sparkled on choppy water and flickered into her eyes. She squinted against the glare, hoping that it didn't set off a megrim. Once or twice since she'd returned to sea, she'd been forced to take to her bed with one of the dreadful headaches. Only darkness and sleep seemed to rid her of it. She scowled at the sparkling waves—resenting anything that kept her from enjoying flying across the waves with the wind. She licked the salt from her lips and closed her eyes, letting the ocean's movement beneath the ship sooth her.

The next day, they rounded the tip of La Florida and anchored offshore where Rosso and Paddy supervised loading the pinnace.

Capulet looked torn between staying and going, but after pumping Rosso's hand vigorously, he followed Romeo to the pinnace.

Anne pulled him aside at the rail, "I'll be back this way again, Capulet. If you want, you can join me then. We could surely use a blacksmith."

He nodded eagerly, "I hopes I kin take you up on that. But don' ask for Capulet no more. My momma gave me the name Joseph and I'm takin' it back."

Anne nodded. "That's a good name, Joseph. Keep watch along this stretch of shore then." She proffered a small spyglass.

"I cain't take this!" He shook his head.

"You can and you will. I have another." She grasped his hand and pressed the narrow tube into his palm.

Gingerly, his fingers closed around it. "Thankee." He hesitated for a moment again. "If'n you need a blacksmith, there's a fellow I heard o' on that little French island north o' New York. Name o' Bernard, Eusebe Bernard. He's supposed ta be a dab hand with blades."

"Eusebe Bernard?" Anne touched the dagger at her waist, her eyes widening slightly. EB. Had she just found the blacksmith she'd wondered about for years? Keeping her rising excitement in check, she said, "That's twice now ye've given me useful information; I'm much obliged. I'll be sure to look him up when we're next to New York."

Rosie appeared from where she'd been making her farewells to the few crew members she'd gotten to know. Unexpectedly, she hugged Anne before making her way down the ladder with a sleepy baby strapped to her back. "I won' forgit what you've done for us."

"I wish I could do more." Anne had given them as much as could be spared from the ships' stores, but they would have to find their people on their own. It was common knowledge among the Black people that some of the Indians who had been pushed out of their land by the white settlers were hiding in La Florida's thick jungle along with a number of escaped slaves. Rosso, and the other freed slaves among the crew, had also heard these rumours, though they had no clear idea of where the settlements could be found. And, of course, none of the white sailors on board had even heard the tales to begin with, leaving Romeo and his small family to find the way themselves. They were on their own.

Anne didn't stay to watch the pinnace row ashore nor its return. She disappeared into her cabin, eager to chart the next leg of their journey: back to Nassau to find her firstborn, hunt down those rumours of her missing son, and hopefully discover who had stolen the other half of her beloved Mary's heart. And maybe make a little profit while she was there; she had to dock long enough to let Clive sell something before the poor man burst.

Twenty Years Gone

The morning they arrived back at Nassau was stormy, matching Anne's vile temper. She'd had barely gotten a wink of sleep—her monthlies had made a long overdue appearance, ending her hope she'd shifted to crone and could put away her rags. She'd spent the night curled into a ball around the pain in her belly, alternating sips of willow bark tea from Cookie or bumbo and trying to ignore Alexandra, who had spent the night vomiting into a bucket.

The third time the green-faced lass used the bucket, Anne had snapped. "You'd better not be with child or you're off my ship until you've had it. A ship is no place for a baby." A vivid memory of Blackbeard saying something similar to her flashed into her mind, making her shiver.

Alexandra had sworn she was sick from eating a bad oyster, but only time would tell if the lass was lying. Anne would be happy when the hold was partitioned off so the girl could have her own space and not be under Anne's feet all the time. She'd have to light a fire under Rosso to get that done soon.

Groaning as she dragged her achy body from bed, Anne looked over at the young woman, sprawled asleep in front of the desk. It had become obvious to Anne over their two months at sea that the lass had a secret, but as long as it didn't impede her work or produce a babe, she could keep her silence. Anne had known many secretive people over the years, including Calico. The only time he'd shared one of those secrets with her was after they'd played the two-backed beast while he was too sleepy to guard his tongue. She shook her head, dispelling the memory and the questions of whether the lass was with child and whose it might be.

Stepping over the girl's arm where it was flung out from under the desk bolted to the decking, she made a mental note to ask Paddy to string up a hammock until the girl's cabin would be finished. Alexandra couldn't keep sleeping on the floor. It was bad enough she must share her quarters—Anne was tired of walking over the young woman's sprawled limbs each morning. At least the lass's clothes were out of sight in a drawer under the captain's bed.

She slid open one of her own clothing drawers. Grumpily, she plucked up the stays, petticoats, and gown neatly folded inside, wishing she could wear her usual loose shirt and pants. Since the day she'd stepped foot onto *Anne's Revenge* nearly two months earlier, she'd only worn the dress once to visit the admiral. But she would never forget how it felt to restrain her body, her voice, and her every move while living with her father.

Today, she was looking for answers, though, and it was sometimes easier to get those answers when you were perceived as weak rather than forceful. A pirate captain inspired fearful cooperation, but, for today at least, that fear would be at the expense of the answers she sought. A skirt and bodice were the simplest solution to appear in need of assistance and helpless, even if she despised wearing them.

"It's only for a day," she muttered and stomped out of the cabin, a hat swinging from one hand and her reticule containing her son's miniature looped over her other wrist.

The sky was darkened by clouds, and in the distance, she could see rain sheeting down, although it was not raining where she stood. Damp patches on the decking showed they'd caught some of the rain earlier. Black Brian and Little Titch were still mopping up puddles at the bow.

The rest of the crew crowded between the two hatches where Big Titch was divvying out shares to the crew. Half the crew would soon disappear into the brothels and alehouses lining the piers while the others remained aboard waiting their turn.

She stalked around them as best as she could while in skirts to join her first mate over by the pinnace, ignoring the startled looks at her attire from some of sailors who'd never before seen her in women's garb. Rosso gave her a sidelong glance, then turned back to Clive and Paddy, who leaned over the railing, his lengthening curls trapped in a queue at his neck, watching the pinnace lowering on its hooks.

Wisely, none of them said anything about her skirts.

"We'll be docking later this morning. We're just waitin' on a ship to leave their berth." Rosso said, "I thought ye'd like an early start rather than waitin' so we've made a pinnace ready for ye."

Anne nodded. "Thank ye." She glanced over the railing at the nearby dock and the village beyond it.

Nassau had changed quite a lot since she'd last been there. Raw wood showed on the docks where repairs had been made over the years, and there was a new building for the harbourmaster. The biggest change was to the village beyond. She remembered a small derelict collection of buildings that could generously be called huts. A few were still scattered around, but now the greater part of the village was comprised of neat one- or two-story wooden buildings in tidy rows along the dirt roads. Some were obviously small family homes, and others were as large as manufactories. Behind them stood even more structures hazy in the morning fog that hadn't yet burned off.

Nassau had grown into quite a large community, nothing like the ramshackle village she'd known, full of raucous pirates spending their plunder in the alehouses and brothels. A brief nostalgia for its loss came over her.

She climbed down the rope ladder into the pinnace, wondering if she'd know anyone here. Twenty years was a long time to be away. She twisted her distinctive dark red hair up and plunked her wide-brimmed hat over it, just in case anyone here remembered a particular red-haired pirate lass after all these years. That was the other reason why she was wearing women's clothing, to hide her identity. Her belly cramped again, and she placed a soothing hand there.

The crewman assigned to the pinnace's oars pulled strongly, and the shore drew closer minute by minute, barely giving Anne time to think. She still hadn't decided on a course of action after today. She hadn't been able to focus on it. It was hard to think past the idea that she might meet her long-lost child today. The idea made her more nervous than any battle ever had, and her belly pains were an oddly welcome distraction from her worries.

A short while later, the pinnace bobbed at the dock. Leaving Paddy and Clive to bring up the rear, she walked along the muddy rutted path leading into town, Rosso a half step behind her as usual. Behind them, in a low voice, Paddy gave last-minute instructions to Clive, who was charged to ask around for the various items on James Bonny's list.

As they came closer to the village proper, the streets began to fill with men, women, and children beginning their day. They eyed her and the three men with mild curiosity.

Anne adjusted her hat and tucked a strand of hair back under the wide brim. She half turned away from the passersby, hiding her face by pretending to speak to Rosso. She had to snap her fingers at him to get his attention, as his eyes kept dropping to her bosom. The ridiculous stays respectable women were expected to wear had an advantage she'd used many times to her benefit—it pushed her bosoms into view. It amused her how easily men were caught by the sight of a little cleavage. As soon as the pedestrians passed, she turned from the bemused Rosso and focused on her own task, finding the right Watling family.

The Watling distillery wasn't on the main island where she stood. It was on a smaller island further south, but a few branches of the family lived here as representatives of the rum distillers. One of the powder monkeys, Abernathy, had grown up on Nassau and said there were four houses of Watlings here. One was a bachelor the last he'd heard but the others were larger. He'd drawn the rough map that Rosso now carried in a pocket, showing the locations. Hopefully, one of them had taken her child in.

She mentally rehearsed how to introduce herself. She'd spent the previous night, between Alexandra's vomiting sessions and her own agonizing cramps, considering the best way to broach the subject of mislaid infants with whomever she found at home.

Clive peeled off, heading for the island's largest tavern where he'd start asking after James Bonny's goods. Anne and the others continued on through the town and along a tree-lined path.

Anne's heart beat a little quicker as they neared the first of the three Watling houses. They were in a small enclave separated from the rest of the town by a wide road. The dwellings were large, white-painted and airy places, fitting for the rum barons who lived there. Neat gardens of flowering bushes surrounded two of the three buildings.

The first one was empty, abandoned to dust and debris. A number of the windows were broken or framed by crooked shutters, and the front door was shut tightly between two planters choked with dead foliage. Anne shook her head at Rosso when he looked questioningly at her. There was no purpose to knocking—it was evident that it was empty.

The second house was obviously lived-in, so Anne walked up the white crushed-shell path to the front door. Imported rosebushes marched in a row along the front of the house, and the air was thick with their scent.

A man answered their knock. Tall and broad-shouldered, about 30 years of age, he was dressed in shirtsleeves, and his hands were stained with ink. He appeared annoyed to be interrupted, but he answered Anne's questions easily enough. He was the master of the house and the only Watling who lived there, aside from his two elderly servants.

Disappointed by the man's answer, Anne turned to the final house. If this one was not her child's home, then she would have to look further afield at the other Watlings on the smaller islands nearby, which definitely increased the likelihood that her child had not passed a pleasant childhood.

Paddy led the way back to the road and down the next path, this one with pink shells that crunched underfoot. Flower boxes filled with plants native to the island lined the wraparound porch that enveloped the large house, vines erupting from some and making their way up the wooden walls and twining around the windows that faced the road.

Hot from more than an hour's walk in the rising heat, Anne hammered her fist on the third door, once, twice, then three times—an old pirate's signal. She didn't know if these Watlings had ever been connected to any pirates, but it never hurt to keep one's options open.

Footsteps approached the door. Anne's heart beat faster, and her belly spasmed.

One of Each

An elderly Black woman, twice Anne's age, with a face as wrinkled as a raisin, answered the door. *"Bonjour,* can I 'elp you?" Her voice was soft, full of a Bahamian lilt.

"I'm looking for the young master or mistress of the house. I have a message from Charles Towne in Louisiana," Anne said. Oddly, a sudden memory of conversations with the wives of her father's colleagues popped into Anne's mind. She blinked and refocused on the woman in front of her.

The old woman, the housekeeper presumably, looked from Anne to Paddy to Rosso, then back to Anne again to study her closely. Anne was glad she'd left her more piratical garb behind. She quickly understood why she'd remembered those old conversations. Unconsciously, she'd been speaking in the same manner as she'd done when she regularly wore stays and skirts, dropping her natural Irish brogue and using more educated language. She shook off the odd thought yet again.

"Je suis desolée, young Missy ain't 'ere, she's gone 'way. Near four months now." She peered over her shoulder down the hall behind her. "I'm 'appy to take a message for her, but no telling when she'll be back. Since her Papa pass on, she's

been her own mistress, young as she is." There was a twist to the old woman's mouth, half-proud and half-exasperated, Anne saw there was love between them despite her tone.

"How old might young Miss be? We're lookin' for someone of a particular age," Rosso asked.

Anne shot him an annoyed glance for interrupting.

"Miss Johanna's just gone twenty-two. Z'at z'e right age?"

"'Tis indeed, thank ya." Rosso cast a look at Anne.

The full import of the old woman's words hit Anne—her firstborn child was still alive and was a girl. She had a daughter.

A rush of light-headedness swept over her, and, for the first time in her life, she didn't fake swooning; it happened naturally.

"*Sacrebleu!*" The old housekeeper rushed forward at the same time as Paddy, and they knocked into each other while Anne staggered to one side and slid down the wall.

Rosso peered down at her. "Cap..." He shot a nervous look at the housekeeper, who had both hands clutched to her forehead. "Miz Anne? Kin I hep ya up?" He extended his hand, and once Anne's vision had returned to normal, she grasped it firmly as he hauled her to her feet. His hand was warm in hers.

Paddy's chin had a little drip of blood, not enough to do more than spatter his shirt a bit, and the old woman seemed dazed but unharmed. A splotch of blood on her forehead told Anne exactly where she and Paddy had collided.

"What a fine bunch we are!" Wiping her forehead with the edge of her apron, the old woman waved a gnarled hand down the dim hall, "Z'e kitchen, get you cleaned up and give z'is lady someplace to put 'er feet up." She grimaced at the blood spot on her apron.

Within minutes, the three pirates were seated around a massive wooden table, tea cups in hand and a clean rag pressed to Paddy's bloody chin.

"What is z'e message?" The old woman bustled around the airy kitchen, filling a plate with savoury meat tarts from a cupboard.

"I can't say—it was a private one," Anne improvised. She'd assumed her child, her *daughter,* would be here and hadn't thought she'd need a fake message.

"I 'ave seventy-six years now. I knows a lie when I 'ear one." The old woman plunked the plate of tarts onto the table and looked expectantly at Anne.

Anne drummed her fingertips on the table, stalling for time to think.

The housekeeper stared at Anne's moving fingers and then flickered up to Anne's face, widening in sudden recognition. "*Mon dieu!*" She dropped into one of the mismatched chairs at the end of the table. "You're *Missy Johanna's mama!*" She began fanning herself with the bloody end of her apron. Her eyes darted around the table, looking closely at the two men bracketing Anne. Anne realized the old woman knew that Anne had been a pirate long ago and was likely wondering now if she and the men with her still were.

Paddy's rag dropped to the table, and he scraped his chair back, hand going to his sword hilt as he stood.

"Oh, sit down! She's an old woman." Anne snapped at him, but her gaze never left the housekeeper, trying to discern what the old woman thought of Anne being Johanna's mama.

Unfazed by Paddy's sudden move, the old woman smoothed the apron in her lap. "So z'e old bastard is ded, no?"

"What old bastard?"

"Missy's da. Z'e one who stole 'er from you." She grinned broadly, exposing a missing tooth. "I should introduce meself. I'm Constance, I've served z'e Watlings all m' life. I was nurse to Missy Johanna when she got 'ere. Feisty little z'ing. Already angry at z'e world." She raised an eyebrow. "Like her mama, I t'ink."

Anne's lips thinned at the slight insult, or perhaps it was meant for teasing, but she gestured for Constance to continue.

"I always t'ought you'd come looking sumday. I 'member z'e night z'ey brought little Missy in. I know full well she's not z'e Master's. Master Watling swore me ta secrecy so's I couldn't tell Missy her papa was a pirate, but we didn't know nothin' 'bout you. Whyn't you come sooner?"

"My father was poorly, and I didn't know where she was." Anne admitted. As if to make her feel guiltier at abandoning her child, her hip gave a burst of sharp pain. She breathed deeply, through the pain.

Constance touched Anne's hand. "Your girl was raised right. Her fat'er saw to t'at."

"What do you mean?"

"'e may have been a bastard ta take her from you, but 'e looked after 'er. Ever' mont' Master Watling got money. He was one of z'e poor Watlings and z'e only one man enough willing to raise a pirate's child."

"He set up an account for her?" Anne was startled. How had Calico done that? He must have come into some money that she hadn't known about.

The old woman nodded, "Missy was well looked after e'en after z'e money stopped a few years later. Master cared for 'er like 'is own."

Anne stared into her teacup, feeling an unexpected weight lift from her shoulders. Her child had been well looked after and loved.

"I knew nothin' about you but z'at young man knew who she was. Said 'e was 'er brother." She gave Anne a long searching look. "They sure 'nuff looked alike."

Anne's heart pounded with excitement. "A young man came to see her? Is this him?" She unlooped the reticule from her wrist, pulled out the small miniature of Jack, and passed it to Constance.

"Yessir, z'at's Jacques. I wish I had a paintin' of Missy. Z'e one her Papa had was lost when z'e house in Caicos burned down." Constance gently stroked the frame before handing it back to Anne.

A grin bloomed on Anne's face. Jack was alive—both of her children were still alive. She shot a triumphant look at Rosso and Paddy and found them grinning back at her.

She *knew* her son hadn't drowned. She pictured what had happened. Jack had decided to leave the Navy but didn't want anyone to follow him, so he'd pretended to fall overboard. Or maybe he'd stolen the ship. The *Alderborough* had gone missing, after all. She'd told him too many stories about pirates she'd known who'd done that very thing when they couldn't just outright run away.

"When was he here?" she demanded, turning back to Constance.

Constance wrinkled her brow in thought for a moment. "Beginnin' o' June. Z'en 'e an' Missy Johanna lef' a few weeks later."

Three months. Jack was alive as of three months earlier, Anne was giddy at the thought.

Paddy cleared his throat. "Navy told Miss Anne that 'e was lost at sea nearly eight months gone."

"Well, z'ey don't know as much as z'ey t'ink z'ey do." Constance snorted a laugh and shook her head.

"He'll wish he was lost at sea when I catch up to him." Anne lurched to her feet, painful spasms in her hip reminding her to go slower. "Thank you, Constance, I'm much obliged to you."

"When you see my Missy Johanna, tell 'er to come home. Old Constance misses 'er."

"I will, but I doubt she'll listen to me. My son certainly doesn't." Anne scowled and bit back the rest of what she wanted to say.

"Sounds like a family trait." Constance gave her a commiserating smile. "Do your best."

Rosso stood up. "Thank ya kindly for the little pies. They went down a real treat." Anne and Paddy added their own compliments before they took their leave.

Anne strode out of the house with Paddy and Rosso hard on her heels. Now that the excitement of learning she had a daughter was settling into her, she noticed how annoyed she was with Jack. When she caught up to her son, she was going to beat him within an inch of his life for taking such a foolish risk with himself, but mostly, she wanted to smack him for making her think he was dead.

She hurried down the rough and muddy street, itching to be aboard *Anne's Revenge*. The two men brought up the rear, exchanging looks laden with meaning.

"Stop that," she snarled over her shoulder. "I'm thrilled Jack's alive, but I'm still gonna kill him when I catch up to the little bastard. Making me worry for weeks. Sending me on a wild goose chase. God damned little shite." It dawned on her that maybe he'd faked his death so that he could go looking for his sister—that lessened some of her ire. Slightly.

The question now was determining where Jack and Miss Johanna had gone next. Jack had always loved her stories of Calico Jack and the others, from Blackbeard to Charles Vane. He knew where all their favourite Islands were, as Anne herself had told him. If he were hiding anywhere, it would be on one of those Islands. Most likely his father's hiding place, Ragged Island. Calico had loved that island, taking every opportunity to make landfall there.

Anne despised being on land—she felt off balance, not quite herself. At sea, she always knew who she was. It had been damned near perfect, sailing with Calico and Mary, she'd never felt so alive. It was lonely sailing without them by her side, but she was used to being solitary. For the two decades when she had both Da and Jack with her, she'd still felt lonely.

She looked at Paddy and Rosso walking quietly beside her. They were good company as they were, but she needed more than simple friendship to distract her. Fighting was the best diversion she knew, but with her tricky hip, she paid for it in pain the following day. They had a couple of unencumbered days ahead of them waiting for the crew to finish their shore leave. The idea of all those days anchored at port made her skin crawl with restless energy.

Rosso's presence was a solid warmth beside her. She slanted a glance at him, suddenly very aware of the muscles under his linen shirt.

There was something else that relieved that kind of building pressure. Sex.

He looked like he'd know what to do in bed. It had been a while, but she remembered the basics of seduction. She eased her shoulders back a little more, subtly emphasizing her bosom and turned slightly toward him, exaggerating her breathing.

Rosso's eyes dipped down and back up again and then away. Under his dark skin, she glimpsed a blush.

She grinned. It might be she could find some release soon. A warmth spread through her belly at the thought, and her steps became lighter as they walked back through the small community to the docks and *Anne's Revenge*.

The town, if it could be called that, had barely a dozen buildings and it took very little time to walk though it. The success of her mission filled Anne with excitement and purpose—she was finally getting somewhere with her search. Her happiness spilled over, and she smiled and nodded pleasantly to the few people they passed in the street. Rosso shared an exaggeratedly startled look with Paddy at her unaccustomed friendliness, but even that wasn't enough to sour her mood.

Her son was alive, and she had a daughter.

Keeping Trust

In the end, she couldn't follow her desire to depart immediately. For one thing, Clive had threatened to create a ruckus if he weren't able to unload cargo. And the crew would have been in high dungeon if denied shore leave—they took it in turns to visit the brothels and publicans. She hoped they also visited the bathhouses. Some of the men had become quite rank from poor hygiene.

Early morning of their fourth day in port, Rosso badgered her to take one last walk-about before they departed. She'd only gone to stop his jabbering, but at the last, she had to admit she'd enjoyed seeing her old haunts, those that still existed. Continuing her ruse of being a female passenger aboard the *Revenge*, she wore stays and skirts, mildly annoyed over feeling grateful to Clive for taking it upon himself to purchase them without her asking. She almost wished she'd brought some of her own clothing—it fit her much better, for one thing—but at the time, she hadn't expected to wear skirts often, as they were not at all practical aboard ship.

She and Rosso had asked around for a blacksmith willing to go to sea, but none were to be found locally. The plump owner of the nearest inn had regaled her with tales of the very same blacksmith Capulet had told her to hunt down: Eusebe Bernard.

Anne was now utterly convinced this man was the creator of her always-sharp dagger—he apparently possessed a near-miraculous affinity with blades. She'd heard similar stories from nearly half the patrons of the pub. Her own dagger seemed to be the best of his work, and Anne dearly wanted him at her beck and call.

It was near midday when they returned to the docks, and the pleasant taste of beer still filled her mouth from the morning's pint. Before she even set foot on the gangway lowered for her, Rosso bellowed up to the watch, "We leave as soon as Clive and Paddy come aboard!"

Black Brian held on to the end of the gangway as Anne and then Rosso crossed over from the pier to the weather deck.

"Ready sails!" Henry called loudly to be heard above the sound of seagulls squawking over scraps on the beach.

A scrambling of feet pounded across the deck as the crew ran to obey. Anne dodged them and lifted her skirts to climb the steps to the wheel deck.

Henry offered her the wheel, but she shook her head. She leaned on the railing beside him, watching the crew scurry about on the weather deck.

Six unfamiliar faces stared at her from the men lined up to hoist the sails; new recruits picked up in Nassau while she'd been busy with Constance and waiting for Clive and Paddy to sell whatever goods they could. One of them, a terribly thin man, blanched under her gaze. He ducked his head and pulled harder on the sail's rigging. Another one, a dark bearded fellow, preened under her eye and let his lascivious gaze travel over her, head to toe, lingering on her cleavage.

"You! What's your name?" Anne looked him up and down in mocking repetition of his rudeness.

"Robert." He swaggered over to her and bent a leg. "At your..."

"Get off this ship." Henry said flatly. He stood beside Anne, his hands loose on the wheel.

Anne scowled at Henry but kept silent. She was supposed to be a passenger, not the captain.

The grin on Robert's face slipped a notch. "Pardon?"

"I said, get off my ship. Any man who's too busy gawking at a woman to work has no place here."

"But, I..."

Rosso stood near the steps—he was never far away from Anne since Mort's death—and he grabbed Robert's arm to hurry him along.

She looked away from the unfortunate Robert. A frozen figure caught her eye. Alexandra stood still, staring at Anne with a strange look on her face.

"Is there something you want to say?" Anne lifted an eyebrow at the young woman. What had gotten into the lass? Had she never seen Anne in skirts before? Clive had bought the clothing in Nassau. If she remembered correctly, the girl came from nearby. Perhaps she'd known the skirt's previous owner? Whichever it was, the lass needed to learn how to hide her thoughts better. A pirate, particularly a woman, needed more control.

Alexandra shook her head. "No, ma'am." She scurried off to take Robert's place at the sails.

A loud yelp ending with a splash came from dockside. Robert had departed the ship.

Rosso popped his curly head over the steps to the wheel deck. "Anythin' else I can do for ya, Cap'n?"

"Not at the moment, Rosso."

"Ya're getting soft. Was a time you'd have just stabbed any man looked sideways at ya."

Anne's mouth dropped open, and she grabbed for the knife, which was usually snugged behind her sash, before she remembered she'd left it in her cabin, along with her usual clothes.

"I'm jus' sayin'." Rosso tipped his hat to her and sauntered down the weather deck, heading to the bow.

She frowned after him. "Are ye offering to let me sheath my knife in ye for practice?"

He laughed and continued walking. Anne shook her head, bemused, her annoyance derailed by his cheek.

Clive and Paddy pounded up the gangway. As soon as they set foot aboard, Black Brian pulled the long board back and stowed it away. Clive and Paddy went to join Anne and Henry on the wheel deck.

"Glad ta see ye finally came back. We kin sail now," Anne greeted them.

"Are ye mad?" Paddy demanded, looming over Anne despite being nearly the same height, "There'll be mutiny if'n we leave now!"

"Tha rest o' tha men'll be 'ere soon," Clive said quietly.

Anne snorted. "We've been at sea for barely a fortnight since our last landfall, and they've had near four days shore leave and shares. They've got the best rum for rations, and

Cookie's feeding 'em well. D'ye really think they're hard done by?"

Paddy groaned. "Dammit. They ain't all had shore leave, ye daft..." he trailed off.

She gave him a long hard look at his near slip before she turned to Clive. "Did you get some of those items for Bonny?"

He nodded, his fair hair flopping over his eyes. "A couple and a few more'll be here in a week or two—we kin come back for those. I sold some o' tha cotton and most o' tha flour, if'n we can stay long enough ta unload."

"We catch the next tide."

"'Tis almost evenin' tide now. Gimme tha mornin' tide, fourteen hours. Ye give me those hours, and I'll offload tha rest while waitin'," Clive promised.

"Deal." She shook his ink-stained hand and watched him leave before turning to Paddy. "If you think anyone will be sober enough to work tomorrow you kin let the rest o' the crew ashore tonight."

Paddy looked startled but pleased as well, "You're mad, completely mad. Sail drunk? Do ye think they're ever sailin' sober? Mad Annie suits ye." He shook his head and disappeared into his cabin.

Anne laughed. He had a point. A great deal of rum was consumed by sailors of any rank, herself included. Suddenly thirsty, she headed to her own cabin for a drink and to divest herself of her skirts.

"Hoist tha mains'l!" Paddy called out in the dim light before dawn. Instantly, the grunting of fifteen men, and one woman, pulling halyards filled the air.

The ship shuddered beneath Anne's feet as the canvas caught the wind, snapping the sails taut.

"Cap'n? What's ma headin'?" Paddy's voice was soft, just loud enough to hear.

"New York. But I want ye ta take a heading ta Ragged Island first." It was the nearest island she thought might be Jack's hiding place. She had a list of other possibilities, but this was the one she'd spoken of most often when Jack wanted stories.

"Aye, aye."

The swells dancing beneath the hull sent shivers through Anne's feet. She curled her toes into the dew-damp wood of the deck. Staring off to the east where the sun was just lifting over the horizon, she considered what to do with her son when she caught up to him and his sister.

Paddy cleared his throat.

"Would ye stop doing that? Just speak if ye got something ta say," Anne snapped.

Paddy grunted, "Are ye sure you want ta go inta business wit' Bonny? He was a damned traitor." He hawked over the railing.

There was a long moment of silence while they each remembered lost friends and lovers.

"He says he weren't." There was another long pause before Anne continued, "I don't know tha' I believe him, but tha' was twenty years ago. He's a merchant now, and we have a lot o' wares ta sell."

"Do ye trust him that much?"

Anne harrumphed. "I don't trust him as far as I could throw him. He's useful, is all."

"All right then."

A tiny mewling sound came from the middle of a coil of cable flung over the belaying pins behind the wheel. Anne turned to peer into the shadow. A dark furry animal peered out at her.

"Do we have a rat problem?" Anne squinted at the fuzzy brown creature.

"Not anymore." Paddy kept scanning the horizon as they slipped away from shore. "Rosso foun' a kitten in a box on the docks. All t'others died. Its mam is down wit' tha ballast stones taking care o' tha rats. Rosso said to give this one ta ye."

Anne crouched down to stare at the tiny thing. Its ears were perky little triangles. Tiny claws scrabbled for purchase on the thick coils of rope before the kitten fell backward onto its tail, another mew escaping it.

She bent forward to pluck it out of its nest. "So, what's your name?" Deep brown eyes stared up at her. It was mottled with patchy shades of brown and gold all over, with a lighter spot on its belly. A tiny pink tongue peeked out as it yawned, then it snuggled into her bosom. She let it stay there, its rumbling purr feeling good against her chest. Her deep anger at Jack's deception began to drain away.

He must have had reason: she hadn't raised a callous man. Difficult as it was, she had to trust him. She stared out to the horizon.

The future stretched out ahead of her, so full of possibilities she felt young and giddy. Now that she'd gotten her sea legs back, the idea of returning to Carolina, whether to live there or only visit, was horrifying.

She took a deep breath of the salt air. She wanted to stay exactly where she was. There was no corset binding her to domesticity, no shoes mincing her footsteps, and no man stopping her from laughing or fighting. She could even find a lover if she wanted—Da wasn't here to disapprove.

Unbidden, her gaze travelled the weather deck until she found the broad-shouldered Rosso watching her. She nodded thanks for the kitten in her arms. He flashed a quick smile before turning back to his conversation with Henry.

He'd be a good lover, Anne knew. Strong and thoughtful, even Calico Jack wouldn't have faulted her choice. He wasn't afraid of her like half the men she met. He gave her the rough side of his tongue when she deserved it, but never talked down to her like her father's colleagues had done. Of all of the men aboard, he was the only one that she felt comfortable with in the way of women with men. He was born a slave but hadn't been raised one. He had no family nearby, but his sisters lived in Upper Canada. He hadn't offered any more information than that.

The first rule she'd learned at sea was not to ask questions of another. A man's stories, or woman's, were offered freely or not at all. A smile lifted her lips at the thought that perhaps she would learn more of Rosso on her pillow if she could ever get the man there. He seemed oblivious to her recent flirtations, but she knew how to tempt a man even if she'd not used those skills for many years.

Movement on the weather deck caught her eye—Alexandra swarming up the rigging, her earlier sick stomach forgotten.

That morning, Anne had finally seen the young woman's rag strips hanging in a hidden corner of the captain's cabin, putting her worries to rest—the lass wasn't expecting a child.

Seeing the lass reminded her. "Did Clive get me the boards I wanted ta build the lass her own cabin below?"

"Ayup. I'll set a couple o' men to work with Alex soon as we're at sea. Ye'll have yer cabin to yerself soon."

The tiny kitten in Anne's arms yawned and stretched. She stroked its furry head and smiled at Rosso, imagining him in the bed of her soon-to-be private cabin. It was unlikely that she would have to worry about babes much longer, being so close to the Change, but Cookie had the right herbs to prevent it from lodging in the first place. She'd made sure the lass knew of them.

The kitten squirmed again, seeking attention. His calico coat ruffled in a breeze.

"Shall I call you Calico?" He'd have gotten a right laugh at her naming a cat for him and his habit of wearing clothing that caught attention.

The kitten blinked at her. Anne stroked its tiny head and looked out to sea, the salt wind in her face and the rolling waves beneath her lending her some much-needed peace. She never wanted to live on land again. She would have to visit her father's home at least one more time since she had promised Sara to come back for her. But the sea was her home.

How could she ever return to a place that treated her as less than she was? Discounted her at every step, denied her autonomy? She was a captain, a leader of men, and the sea was her place.

She simply needed to figure out how to tell her son. And her daughter—she had no idea what her eldest child thought of her, whether she'd prefer her mother on land or at sea. She gazed out over the water and tried to imagine what the lass would look like and who she might resemble in character as well as in physique.

The Chase

Footsteps running overhead woke Anne from a deep sleep. She leaped out of bed, tangled hair flying wild around her face. "Bloody hell, what's going on up there?" She reached for her trousers.

In the hammock swinging over the table, Alexandra grunted and rolled over.

Shouts echoed through the short passageway just outside her cabin. Before Anne had even pulled her boots on, her door creaked open.

"Cap'n Anne?" a hoarse whisper came from the dimness—Rosso.

"What's happened?"

"A ship. They ain't showing their colours. 'Bout 1200 yards away. Almost cannon range," Rosso said.

"God dammit!" Anne brushed past him in the doorway, suddenly acutely aware of the heat of his body. She shook off the thought and said, "All hands on deck, Alex. Kick her if she don't move, Rosso."

"No need, I'm awake," Alexandra said from the darkness.

The moon was up but shed little light, and the sun hadn't yet breached the horizon. Anne could see two small dots of yellow light bobbing on the ocean behind them, playing peekaboo behind the waves. Still a long distance away, but closing on them.

She loped up the wheel deck steps right behind Rosso. Henry and Paddy stood there already, Henry's hands on the wheel and Paddy peering through the brass spyglass. He handed it to Anne.

"You'll want ta fetch more cannon balls," Rosso said to Paddy, recently promoted to weapons master in addition to his bosun duties.

Small crates of balls rested beside each of the six-pounder cannons already, but they would likely need more. Paddy nodded and sprinted down to the forward hatch, bellowing to Little Titch and Black Brian. Fetching the cannon balls was a cabin boy's duty.

Anne glanced down in time to see Alexandra disappearing down the hatch, joining the lads crewing the two port-side cannons.

A movement by one of the other ship's masts caught her eye. She squinted into the darkness. "Is that a flag going up?"

Peering through the spyglass lens, she could see the flag, but not the markings or colours in the darkness. From their foreshortened view of the other vessel's bow she couldn't even see what size the flag was. "I don't..."

Rosso tried to yank the spyglass from Anne's hand. "Ya cain't see the broadside o' a barn. Both masts are square-rigged, it's a brigantine. They're British, I see wigs."

Anne smacked Rosso's hand away and pulled the spyglass back to her face. Focusing on the other ship's deck, she could just make out two figures at the wheel, white-wigged heads and metal buttons shining in the moonlight. "Wigs. At sea. Bloody idiots."

Rosso snorted and shrugged, "They're English."

"How long before they've caught us up?" Anne handed the spyglass to him.

"Half hour, they've got more sail aloft than we do." Henry replied. He looked calm.

"Yell for me if they start talking with their little flags." Anne hurried off to fetch her pistols and bag of shot—she'd likely need it before long.

The sun was just peeking over the horizon, back-lighting the English brigantine, when Anne reappeared up top, buckling her pistol belt around her waist.

"We've some time," Henry said from behind the wheel. "Rosso's fetching food, if you're hungry."

Anne shook her head and peered into the eastern sky. "A quarter hour. They'll reach us at true sunrise then."

Henry sniffed, "Think they planned it?"

"Might be. I'd have done the same if I wanted to board a ship."

Footsteps behind them announced Rosso's return. He handed Anne a small loaf of bread, then ripped the larger one in half and offered one piece to Henry.

Absentmindedly, she pulled a bite off as she resumed peering at the oncoming ship. The weight of her pistol and the sword tucked into her sash felt reassuring.

"Have they sent a message yet?" Rosso mumbled around the bread.

His own mouth full, Henry shook his head in answer.

"Nearly in cannon range now," Rosso said.

A motion in the thick patch of darkness that was the other ship made Anne peer closely and then choke on the bread. She spat out the wet wad. "Sweet Jesus! They're crossing the T!"

The brigantine was swinging ponderously around and bringing its starboard-side cannons into position for firing on *Anne's Revenge.*

"Master at arms! Ready!" Rosso bellowed.

Henry wrenched the wheel around, turning the ship to make a narrower target.

A hollow boom came across the water, closely followed by a high-pitched whistling.

Paddy roared orders to his cannon crew. The main deck was a flurry of motion as the powder monkeys set to work and the rammers stood by. Paddy crouched behind the first cannon, checking the angle. "Hold 'til we turn, ye whoresons!" He rushed to the second portside cannon as a huge gout of water geysered up a few yards off the bow.

More cannon blasts thundered across the water.

Anne's knuckles turned white on the railing, squashing the forgotten bread in her hand. "How many per side?" she called over her shoulder to Rosso, who still had possession of the spyglass.

"Ten. Twenty-four pounders." His voice was tight. A twenty-four-pound shot would easily break a hole in the hull, shatter a mast into splinters, or punch a hole through the weather deck.

Anne shuddered at the idea of her beloved *Revenge* being damaged.

A double gout of water splashed astern.

"Two and three," Alexandra counted off, telling Paddy which cannons on the other vessel were ready to fire.

"Take the wheel!" Henry yelled at Rosso before he dashed to the railing where he could see better. "Get that jib down!"

Rosso tossed the spyglass to Anne as another cannon ball whistled on its way. His biceps bunched as he spun the wheel rapidly.

The shot went wide again, but only barely. It hit close enough to splash water onto the *Revenge*'s deck.

"Do it now, Henry," Anne said quietly in the silence. Over the weeks of sailing, she, Mort, Henry, and Rosso had devised responses to various situations; this was one they'd discussed.

"Loosen all sail!" Henry shouted. The plan was to slow them enough that Paddy would have a brief moment to fire. Hopefully his aim was true.

The wind luffed out of the sails, and *Anne's Revenge* heeled over sharply, tilting the deck beneath Anne's feet. As the ship's wallow steadied, Paddy gave a sharp whistle—the signal to fire.

The first loud boom came from the *Revenge's* forward portside cannon. A crunching noise followed immediately and a scream of pain with it.

Rosso cursed under his breath. "I told 'im to make sure the ijits moved out of the way."

The smell of gunpowder was thick and acrid, billowing out of the hatch. Without looking, Anne knew the cannon had skidded off its tracks and slammed into one of the cannon crew, either a powder monkey or the striker. "They sure as hell know now," Anne said. Ignoring the gurgling screams below deck, she kept her eyes trained on the other ship, waiting. The *Revenge's* shot splash into the water a short distance away from the other ship.

"Ten yards!" she called to Paddy.

An answering thunder came from the pursuing vessel.

"Five and six!" Alexandra shouted.

"Up two degrees!" Paddy whistled again, and their second portside cannon fired.

"Raise sail!" Rosso swung the wheel, "All of them!"

Henry, the sail master, bellowed his own orders and the sails bellied into the wind, yanking the *Revenge* forward as two balls splashed just shy of their port bow.

"Bloody hell, they've caught us up." Rosso slammed a hand onto the wheel. "We don' have a choice, Cap'n. We let 'em board or they blow a hole in us."

Anne scowled, but he was right. They had no choice if they wanted to stay afloat.

Anne unbuckled her pistol belt. She tossed it to Henry with a hard stare. "Do your best to get us free quickly, Captain."

With a grim look, Henry slung the belt around his waist and nodded.

Turning away, she bellowed down the deck, "Alex! Get up here!"

Alexandra skidded to a stop in front of Anne.

"Stay in the background." Anne looked hard at her. "Thank god you've got small bubbies like me. Slouch down to hide what little you got." A sudden thought hit her. "Git to the cabin and hide those rags you left hanging out. No need to let on there's women aboard."

Alexandra nodded, white-faced, and dashed off.

On both hands, Anne slid down the railings of the short ladder to the main deck and landed with a jolt that reawakened the pain in her hip. She limped over to join Paddy. "No more shots. Cap'n Henry's orders!" she told him.

Paddy looked sideways at Anne, who nodded shortly.

Alexandra ran up, panting for breath.

Paddy pushed Alexandra into the rammer's position, "*Andy'll* take over. Give *'im* the ram, Little Titch." The whole crew knew to pretend Anne and Alexandra were men if they were ever boarded by the British Navy.

Little Titch handed Alexandra the long shaft of the ram, then stood looking uncertainly at them. He was skinny and short for his age, and Anne suddenly remembered he was only twelve. She took pity on the youngster's confusion on what he should do and said, "Bring some of those extra cannon balls back down below."

"Aye, Ca... ma'am, I mean sir!" The lad snatched up a ball and ran off.

Anne turned to Paddy, "Keep him out o' sight. I don't want him giving me away to the English."

Paddy nodded and handed her a soft hat from his back pocket.

Regretting that she hadn't yet cut her hair short, Anne tucked her distinctive grey-streaked red locks under the hat, then leaned on the ram and waited, rubbing her aching hip. Her cheeks suddenly flushed with heat. She ignored it and the sweat that trickled down her neck as she watched Henry prepare the ship, *her ship,* to be boarded.

Henry called "Heave too!"

The wind bled out of the sails and *Anne's Revenge* slowed to let the larger brigantine close the distance.

Anne winced. "Dammit."

Paddy touched her on the shoulder. "Ye'll get your *Revenge* back."

She gave him a sharp look for guessing what bothered her the most, then nodded and turned back to the cannon and the pretense that she was a lowly powder monkey. And old and achy powder monkey. She rubbed her hip again.

A Mystery Wrapped

in an Enigma

Keeping her head ducked low, Anne watched the English come aboard. Henry, wearing Captain Kenlock's coat, waited by the stern hatch to greet them, flanked by Rosso, Paddy, and Clive.

Unsurprisingly, she didn't recognize any of the boarders. Once, she'd known by face or reputation many of the captains in his Majesty's navy, but she'd been too long away.

Shadows crisscrossed the *Revenge's* deck from the brigantine's sails looming overhead. Up close, she could see the name painted brightly on the hull: HMS *Enigma*. Some of the three-master's sails were furled to slow them down, and the others billowed in the wind as they kept pace alongside the much smaller *Anne's Revenge*.

"Welcome aboard," Henry said, his gruffness hiding the anger that Anne knew lay beneath.

"Thank you." The insignia on the other Captain's open coat winked in the morning sunshine. He was a craggy old sailor with a ruddy complexion under his wig, and he looked a trifle disheveled. He glanced nervously around the weather deck as the others climbed aboard behind him. The sour smell of cheap rum wafted from his skin.

Anne narrowed her eyes. She exchanged a swift glance with Rosso and knew by his stillness that he'd caught on as well. This man wasn't the captain of the *Enigma*. No captain she'd ever met was a hard drinker: you couldn't keep your crew's respect if you drank more than your ration, and this man's red nose and cheeks, and big belly were mute evidence that he was an admiral of the narrow seas, not Captain of a sailing ship.

"What can I do for you?" Henry said after a long moment.

"I'm Cap'n Smyth, of his Majesty's service." He swept his coat back in a half-bow and pulled a pistol from his belt. "And your cargo is now ours."

Bloody hell and damnation! They're privateers. But why the false captain? From where she stood by the starboard rail, Anne mulled it over.

Henry sighed. "Your writ don't cover me. I'm no enemy to the Crown."

The other man laughed. "You're from those rebellious Colonies, close enough. We have no interest in your little ship. We just want your cargo. Not running was a good beginning. Let's not mess that up, shall we?" He paused, waiting for Henry to nod his head; then, in the overly precise enunciation of a drunkard hiding his intoxication, he said, "What's your cargo?"

"Not much, mostly rum with some flour and cotton," Henry said.

Anne winced. That rum would be worth a fortune in New York. Clive had sold most of the flour and cotton in Nassau and picked up more rum from the proceeds, adding to the barrels they still carried.

"Bloody hell! We've fallen into good luck this morning, gents!" Smyth grinned hugely. He pointed to the gunners' crew, "You lads get started bringing that up and we'll shift it over right quick."

Anne followed the others traipsing to the cargo hold, but she could see no way to avoid losing the rum barrels or the last of the flour. She kept Jack's face in her mind—finding her son and daughter was the goal, along with keeping them safe. But losing her cargo hurt like the very devil. She'd never lost one before. She trudged into the dark hold behind Alexandra and one of the gunnery lads before making a quick detour to the medical stores to scoop up three dark bottles of laudanum. She dug her knife into the lid of the nearest barrel of rum marked as the crew's daily rations and levered the lid up. She emptied one of the bottles into the barrel and hammered the lid back into place. She doctored two others and handed them off to her now-grinning crew to transport above. She then hefted a small but heavy flour bag to her shoulder and made her way up the steps.

A steady parade of sailors muscled barrels and bags to the weather deck, where they were hoisted over the railing and into the tender waiting below.

On Anne's second trip back up the ladder, Smyth called out, "Don't forget your Captain's special hold. He'll have the best liquor tucked away in his cabin for himself."

Anne winced again. She'd gotten used to the best and would miss it of an evening.

She was sweaty and her arms sore by the time she appeared up top with her fourth bag of flour. The tender was gone, taking the first load, including the doctored rum barrels, to the *Enigma* a dozen yards away, so she and Limey and couple of the lads dropped to the deck to catch their breath.

Alexandra appeared in the open hatch and moved to the railing. She dropped the flour bag from her shoulder to the deck beside Anne.

"Where d'ya think y'are? Your momma's parlor? Move yer scrawny arses!" One of the men with Smyth shouted and shoved Alexandra in the back, sending her sprawling to her knees.

Anne saw Alexandra's hands bunching into fists as she glared at him. The brawny man who'd shoved her curled his lip in derision.

Beside Anne, Limey started to move to the young woman's aid.

Anne grabbed his arm and pretended to use it to pull herself upright. "No," she muttered. "It'll go worse for her if they learn she's a woman. Tell her to stay below when she gets back down there." Limey was sweet on the lightning-tempered Alexandra—he'd make sure she stayed away from the *Enigma*'s crew.

He nodded and tugged Alexandra away from the sailor before she could swing her ready fists. Anne sighed with relief when they disappeared below decks again. The lass had a mercurial temper and was still learning when to use those fists and when to refrain.

"Sails ahoy! Two o'clock!" Peg called from the crow's nest.

"'Glass! Bring me a 'glass!" Smyth rushed down the weather deck and flew up the steps up to the wheel and peered at the horizon.

From where he was sitting behind the wheel-spit, Henry spoke. "In my belt." The sailor guarding him yanked the spyglass free and tossed it to Smyth.

"Bloody hell. It's a ship of the line," Smyth muttered. "D'ya see any sails behind it?" His voice slurred a little.

"No, sir! Gotta be a scout though," one of Smyth's crew said, wringing his hands anxiously.

Anne stood near the stern hatch, listening intently. Smyth and his crew were not responding like they'd spied a friend—they were preparing to be attacked exactly as Anne would in their place.

Beside her, one of the *Enigma*'s crew gave a shrill whistle. Across the water, the crew of the brigantine scurried into motion. The three *Enigma* sailors perched in the rigging of *Anne's Revenge* shinnied down the ropes, thumping onto the decks. Midway between the two ships, the tender had reversed direction and was being rowed rapidly back to *Anne's Revenge* to pick up their men, although Anne was certain they hadn't yet had time to unload all the crates of rum bottles they'd been transferring to the *Enigma*.

"Goddam it all ta hell. Back to the *Alderborough!*" Smyth shouted down to the opening in the rail where a knot of his men stood waiting to drop into the tender.

The *Alderborough.* Anne shot a startled look at the brigantine beside her; at the name on its side. Now that she was looking for it, she could see that the name *Enigma* was freshly painted.

Anne leaned against the hatch, her mind racing through the facts: a newly painted ship's name that was so recent a change that the crew still occasionally used the old one, a drunkard for a captain, and, more importantly, a captain and crew who were afraid of other navy vessels.

There was only one conclusion to draw: the HMS *Enigma* wasn't a privateer hiding behind the King's writ saying they could seize an enemy's cargo—they'd gone rogue and become pirates themselves.

Anne began to smile. The *Alderborough* was Jack's ship. She knew who their real captain was, and it wasn't Smyth. It was Jack.

Or at least it had been Jack. She didn't know why this man was pretending to be captain, but she was certain her son had taken the ship for himself. That's why Rear Admiral Harrington was so desperate to find it—he didn't want to lose a ship to pirates on his watch. It would definitely scotch his plans of becoming the next Admiral of the Blue.

Straightening up from her slouch and doffing the cap hiding her red hair, she sauntered up the ladder to the weather deck to Smyth, swaying her hips to emphasize her gender. "It seems to me that you have a problem," she said, using her most authoritative voice to cow the man before her; it had worked on her Da's colleagues.

Turning to face her, he blanched, and his eyes widened in horror. Behind him, Henry struggled to regain his feet, hands tied behind his back.

"Apologies for the subterfuge. I'm Captain of this vessel. Anne Bonny at your service." Anne offered her hand to Smyth.

Henry began to speak, and she raised her other hand to quiet him.

"Jesus Christ, you're Jack's mama!" Smyth blurted out. Hesitantly, he took her hand; his eyes darted around nervously as he shook it.

Up close, the alcoholic fumes coming from his skin were stronger, and it was all Anne could do to not wrinkle her nose in distaste. Instead, she pulled her hand from his damp grasp and forced a grin. "If he's still alive, yes, I am his mother."

Smyth looked from Anne to Henry and back. His shoulders slumped, and he sighed before he replied to Anne's unspoken question. "He's still alive." He smiled uncertainly at her. "Jack left me in charge while he took care of a small errand. I can take you to him."

Anne didn't believe Jack had anything to do with putting this man in charge, but ignored that small problem to deal with later. "We'll discuss that in a moment. Now, as I see it, you need to avoid the Navy, as do I. I propose we play a trick on them." She outlined her plans.

By the time she'd finished speaking, Smyth had regained his colour and was nodding in reluctant agreement.

Behind him, Henry grinned widely. "Mad Annie suits you. This plan is pure madness." He turned to show her his tied hands, and she pulled out her belt knife to cut him free.

"It's only madness if it fails. If it works, ye'll tell me I'm a genius." Anne laughed, letting go of the cultured accent she'd used to cow Symth.

A Play in One Act

Paddy yanked on the rope running up the main mast, pulling the flag down while shouting over his shoulder, "Fetch me tha box o' flags!"

A figure dragged the small battered wooden box out of the wheel deck's storage locker. "Which one, bo'sun?" they said in a gruff voice, keeping their back to the wheel deck and hunching over the box. Anne stared hard at the figure, wondering why they were trying to remain hidden, then recognized who it was: Alexandra. Her lips tightened in displeasure.

"Tha small Union Jack, we're gonna fly our escort's flag just below our own colours."

Anne glanced over from where she stood at the wheel with Smyth and Rosso. She raised her voice slightly to be heard over the sound of the waves slapping the sides of the vessel, "Alex, I don't recall tellin' ye to come above deck."

The young woman's shoulders hunched up further over the box of flags, but she said nothing.

Anne peered sideways at Rosso.

He nodded to Anne in agreement then called down to Alexandra, "We'll have a word tonight."

Alexandra winced. She knew very well that meant a few licks with the strap.

"Wait a minute, Miz Cormac, you can't beat that lad! I sent him to fetch the flags. He was just following orders." Smyth protested.

"That's Captain Bonny, if you please," Anne said, resting a hand on the butt of the pistol in her sash. "And I don't recall asking for your advice in matters of my crew, neither." She gave him a stern look. He'd been sobering up since she'd revealed her identity but had a long way to go before full sobriety.

Smyth's face lost its ruddy hue at the coldness in her voice.

Ever since she'd given him her true name, Smyth had been backtracking his morning's actions. He'd returned the rum and flour still in the tender to the *Revenge's* hold. It was all she could do to prevent him from sending back for the doctored barrels already aboard the *Enigma*. Adding that to the list of things to deal with later, she called out to Paddy, "Put the royal standard up there too. Thinkin' we got royalty aboard will give 'em something else to chew on."

Smyth peered over the railing at his ship. The *Enigma* was a scant hundred yards off the starboard side, leaving *Anne's Revenge* between them and the distant scout vessel, which mostly hid the *Enigma's* bow with its distinctive bowsprit.

"All right then, Captain Smyth, time to do your bit," Anne said.

He nodded and slid down the ladder. Rummaging through the box of neatly folded flags, he pulled out three small ones for Paddy to attach to the second flag pole. Anne frowned a little at his choices. *Merchant, escort,* and *homebound,* he'd said they meant, but she had little way of knowing if they were accurate without a copy of Admiral Vernon's *Fighting Instructions*. Captain Kenlock had been a buffoon to not have his own copy aboard. She'd already spoken to Clive about rectifying the lack but had yet to find another copy outside of the Navy fleet. If there was one aboard the *Enigma*, she would have it copied.

"What are we doin'?" Rosso glared at Smyth's back down below. "Why're we suddenly in league with this... this Englishman?" He put a world of contempt into the word. Anne remembered that he hadn't been with her earlier when she'd unmasked Smyth's subterfuge.

"Did you happen to hear his slip earlier? He called his ship *Alderborough*."

Rosso's eyebrows went up, and he nodded slowly. "Well, then. That puts a different complexion on things. That's your lad's ship, ain't it?"

"Indeed." Anne grinned at him. "And it means as soon as we get rid of tha' scout, we can continue ta Ragged Island or wherever Smyth says Jack is." Lowering her voice, she continued, "We'll need ta keep Smyth and his men aboard. I spiked tha rum casks with laudanum before I knew 'twas Jack's ship." The casks taken first were inferior-grade rum and would have been given to the rank and file in their daily ration. The laudanum would have incapacitated the entire crew without a single shot fired thus allowing Anne time to retrieve her cargo and anything else she took a fancy to.

Rosso snorted with laughter. "I see why ya didn't want those casks back."

"If I'm wrong, and Jack's not in charge o'er there anymore, it'll give us an edge." Certain as she was that this was Jack's command, it would be foolish of her to not make other arrangements.

Paddy raised the signal pole, stretching out the small triangular flags. A tense silence fell as they waited for the far-off scout ship's response.

Henry padded up the steps quietly and came to stand beside Anne. He muttered softly, "I truly hope we're not milking a pigeon here."

Anne suppressed her own disquiet to smile at him, "Smyth won't give us up—he has as much to lose as we do. They'll believe him."

The slap of water against the hull and the wind in the sails kept them company for a bit. Then, at last, movement appeared on the scout ship, flags running up the pole.

Her shoulders tight in anticipation, Anne peered through her spyglass and let out a huff of breath. It was a tiny red triangle. *God speed.*

Muted cheers rose from the crews of both the *Enigma* and the *Revenge,* but Anne didn't stop worrying until the scout vessel had disappeared from view and they had resumed their voyage to Ragged Island.

At a gesture from Rosso, Henry took the wheel, leaving Rosso to follow Anne to her quarters to interrogate Smyth and find out exactly where her son was hiding. "Smyth! Get yer arse to ma cabin!" She stepped down the steep stairs lightly, eager for the upcoming discussion.

From the stricken expression on Smyth's face, he was not as eager, but he followed her nonetheless.

"Land ho!" Big Titch's voice floated down from the crow's nest through the still air.

Anne hurried up the narrow passageway from her cabin and into the bright patch of sunlight on the weather deck. She shaded her eyes and called for a passing sailor to fetch her hat from the wardroom where she'd last seen it. Her boot heels thumped on the wooden decking. Her feet felt oddly constrained by the well-fitting boots—she'd been barefoot for weeks aboard ship, save for her visits ashore in Nassau and New York. "What's tha time?" she called out to Rosso behind the wheel.

He tipped his head and squinted up at the shadow of the mast crossing the deck, "Three o' the clock."

The sun glanced off the bobbing water, sending splinters of light into Anne's eyes. The island only a short distance across the water looked abandoned, but she knew it wasn't. She could feel the weight of eyes watching them from the treeline.

"Lower the pinnace," she said, "and pick out enough men to fill it."

Rosso grinned at her. "Aye, Mad Annie. What about Smyth and his men?"

She gave him a sidelong glance at the nickname. "Ask Smyth to join us." The *Enigma* had anchored a little further into the cove, lowering their tender to ferry a number of people ashore to replenish their water barrels.

Smyth hadn't yet gone ashore, and she didn't want him with her when she saw her son again. There was something about the man that itched at her. She'd pulled quite a bit of information from him with Rosso's assistance, but her natural inclination was to distrust the man.

His story about how Jack had come to be in command of the newly renamed *Enigma* was so farfetched as to be nearly unbelievable. He claimed that Jack had been accosted by the Commander, and he'd knifed the man in retaliation. When their Captain said that Jack would be court-martialed for buggery, Jack had used his popularity with the underofficers and the crew and tossed the Captain and Commander overboard.

Anne shook her head. If Rear Admiral Harrington was correct, Jack was about to be elevated to lieutenant commander, making him third in command of the vessel despite his youth. What had happened with the Commander to make him act so rashly? And why had he left Smyth in charge of the Enigma? What was he doing on Ragged Island?

The sun was warm on her bare head. Rosso stepped away from the wheel, his hand coming to rest on the cutlass hanging from his waist. He turned to grin at Anne before bellowing, "Henry! Get yer backside over here!" Calling a half dozen other names, he handed the wheel to Henry and strode off.

Anne licked the salt spray off her lips and stared at the island. Somewhere in that mess of trees, she was sure that Jack stood watching her. Perhaps her daughter was there too.

It had been more than a year since she'd seen him and nearly a month since she'd been given word he'd been lost at sea. She was trying to contain her excitement, and her anger at being lied to, but it was getting more difficult by the moment.

Heat under her palm drew her attention downward. She'd somehow walked to the sun-warmed hand cannon on the left bow and pulled the ignition pin back, ready to load. "Damn my eyes, I'm not going to shoot my son! No matter what he's done." She shook her head and stomped to her cabin, her hand now unconsciously gripping the pistol hanging at her waist.

The *Alderborough* was slightly ahead of them, blocking her view of the western part of Ragged Island. Anne couldn't see around the other ship, but she remembered the island well from her long-ago visits with Calico. There was a small cove hidden there, not quite deep enough for a two-master but plenty big enough for a slew of smaller boats. If she were hiding on this island, that small cove was where she'd have offloaded and then sent the large brigantine around to the far side of the island out of sight of the main shipping lanes.

Smyth joined her at the railing. Sweaty and reeking of alcohol again, he was quite obviously terrified of Anne. She rather enjoyed his terror—it made up at least a little for the embarrassment of being boarded by the *Enigma* in the first place. She didn't speak to him, letting him stew in his fear.

Hell and damnation, she was a pirate—*she* was supposed to do the boarding. One hand on her pistol and the other on her sword, she swayed with the movement of the deck beneath her feet.

She would soon see her tricky son. She looked forward to hearing *his* explanation of how he'd acquired one of His Royal Majesty's vessels. She cast a stern look at Smyth. His story couldn't possibly be correct.

"You'll stay here while I'm ashore." She didn't want his presence to distract Jack or herself during their reunion, as she was convinced that he'd somehow taken charge without Jack's leave. Even if he hadn't, she would much prefer privacy to tell Jack that his second in command was a drunkard.

He nodded jerkily. "As you command."

The shore drew near. Anne ignored the panting of the sweaty oarsmen behind her and peered at the shadows under the trees. A faint movement soon resolved into shimmery figures walking out into the bright sunshine. Two people. There was no way to judge height or build at this distance, but Anne's breath caught in her throat. *Jack!*

Her eyes never left the figures as the pinnace came close enough that the bottom scraped the sand.

"Pull 'er in!" Rosso ordered, and four of the crewmen splashed over the side and waded to shore, towing the light vessel in closer.

Anne felt a hand on her arm, preventing her from rising. Her eyebrows raised, and she gave Rosso a startled look. He'd never voluntarily touched her before, at least not with the crew to see.

"A minute, Cap'n," he said. "Now's the time, lads."

A gap appeared between two of the men clutching the sides of the pinnace. In a practiced motion, a wet plank was lifted from brackets bolted to the outside of the pinnace. One end of the long plank was slipped into a groove along the forward rail with the far end resting on the beach: a walkway for the captain.

Rosso leaped into the water and offered her his arm. Apparently, she was to arrive in style. The pinnace bobbed in the surf when she rose to her feet, and she lightly rested her hand on Rosso's arm as she stepped up onto the plank. The wet board bounced a little under her feet when she started walking above the water. She kept her gaze trained on the two figures waiting on the beach.

Ragged Island

The sun beat down on Anne's bare head and bounced sparkles of light from the water. From the elevated plank, she could see the two people on the beach had come close to the water while her view had been blocked. She could make out their faces now.

The man was definitely Jack. She drank in her son's features: the crooked smile just like his father's, the brown eyes crinkling in the bright sunshine. A lock of wavy dark hair fell into his eyes just as it had when he was a child, long enough to tell her he hadn't cut his hair since his supposed drowning. Clad in his dark blue naval uniform with the jacket undone in the heat, he looked good—healthy and strong.

She gave a curious look at his companion. A dark-haired and buxom young woman, she was as tall as Jack and wore men's clothing with a cutlass on one hip and a pistol on the other. Anne felt a pang of disappointment that the woman didn't resemble Calico or herself in the slightest degree, and the faint hope that this was her daughter faded away. She turned back to Jack, knowing that the men with her, especially Rosso, would keep watch on the stranger.

"Mama!" Jack opened his arms wide as she strode across the wet sand to him, followed closely by Rosso and Paddy.

Anne filled her eyes with her son's visage, revelling in his presence. Swinging her arm wide, she backhanded him across the face, sending him flying onto his backside in the white sand.

Gasps came from every throat around her.

Anne stepped forward to where her son lay, dazed, and grabbed a fistful of his shirt front. "Be thankful I don't shoot ye for scaring me like tha'," she growled.

Jack blinked and peered up at her. "I missed you too, Mama." Grasping Anne's arm, he pulled himself to his feet. The imprint of a red hand blossomed on his cheek. "Can I hug you now?"

In answer, Anne wrapped her arms around him and tucked her head under his chin. "Don't ever do that again," she snarled against his shirt. She squeezed tightly, and he did the same.

"I am sorry, Mama. I thought you'd guess the truth right away. I didn't think you'd believe I drowned." Jack said.

"Of course, I didn't believe it, but I wasn't sure now, was I?" Anne pulled back and examined his face, his brow furrowed with contrition. "Why didn't you tell me you'd gone looking for your sister? I'd have gone with you."

A throat-clearing cough came from his companion. Anne turned to look at the woman standing with Jack. Up close, she examined the young woman's features again for similarities to Jack or Calico but found none. "Are you..."

The young woman shook her head and stuck out her hand. "No, ma'am. I'm not Jack's sister. I'm Charlotte, Charlie to my friends. You knew my mum, Mary Read."

Anne gasped in shock and then a wave of heat blasted through her, pinking her ears and raising all the hair on her arms. "My father told me you died at birth." She searched Charlie's face for signs of her old friend and occasional lover but found none. She must have taken after her father, Mark, but Anne couldn't bring his face to mind, it had been too many years since she'd seen him last.

Charlie shook her head, short dark hair swinging. "Sorry to say this, but your papa fibbed."

Anne could believe that, as her father would have done any amount of lying to prevent her from returning to the sea. If she'd known Mary's child was alive, Anne would have gone looking to be sure the babe was well taken care of. She'd already had to leave one child behind; it would have been impossible to leave a second, especially Mary's. To Jack, she said, "So where's yer sister, then?"

"Captain," a soft voice said behind her, "I'm Jack's sister."

Anne spun around, sand spraying out from under her feet.

It was Alexandra.

The lass stood quietly in front of Anne for a long moment. Only the drumming of the young woman's fingers on her thighs betrayed her nerves. She met Anne's gaze directly. "Johanna Alexandra Cunningham Watling, at your service." She nodded, a short jerky motion. Her face was pale under her newly acquired tan.

Anne's own hands clenched into fists, and it was an effort to loosen them.

Paddy peered at the young woman and stepped back, shaking his head slightly. "I shoulda known. Ye got so much o' yer daddy in ye, I missed seeing tha little bits o' yer mama."

Anne stared hard at Alexandra. Until now, she hadn't even noticed the young woman had been on the pinnace—she'd been so focused on the island and seeing Jack again.

"Don't be angry at Jack. I made him promise not to tell you he'd found me." Alexandra swallowed visibly. "I wanted to get to know you first, before you knew who I was. That's why I sent you the message—I wanted you to go to sea so I could join your crew."

"So, you lied," Anne said flatly. "You both lied to me." She glanced back at Jack who grinned unrepentantly, his cheek still flaming with her handprint.

"Mama, I should've told you, but honestly, didn't you have fun solving our riddle?" Jack said lightly, but the worried line across his forehead showed he wasn't quite as calm as he pretended.

Anne took a deep breath. Her heart felt full to bursting. Not only was her son not dead like she'd feared, he'd planned this reunion with her lost daughter and somehow found her beloved Mary's daughter too. All while getting her to return to the sea. Jack had always known she'd only stayed on land to please her father, although he'd never known of William Cormac's threat to send him away to boarding school if she disobeyed. She was thrilled to see Jack and so angry with him she could spit nails.

And yet all that paled to the emotions flooding her as she stared at Alexandra. This was the child she'd always regretted leaving behind and hadn't truly believed until this moment that she'd see them again.

Her daughter.

The subtle similarities the young woman shared with Calico sprang into sharp focus. Anne suddenly knew why she'd been missing Calico so much recently when she'd barely thought of him in years. It hadn't been because she was at sea again—she'd been reminded of him every time she laid eyes on their daughter. Alexandra was his child far more than hers.

She'd spent weeks sharing a cabin with this young woman and hadn't known, hadn't guessed, hadn't bloody well recognized her own child. How could she have not known?

Stepping forward, Anne raised her hand to Alexandra's cheek. She'd meant to touch it gently, yet somehow her hand had other ideas and slapped the young woman.

"I told you what would happen if I ever caught you lying to me again."

Alexandra flushed, and Anne saw her hands curl into fists. "I deserved that. But you will never strike me again."

For the first time, Anne saw a hint of herself in the young woman, the spine of steel grown from living in a man's world and being expected to be decorative and not functional. To make yourself smaller.

"I never strike without reason. Ask your brother." A quiet thrill of joy spread through Anne from using the words 'your brother.'

Jack nodded. "Mama's got a temper, but she gets over it quick."

Anne had to laugh. "That's true enough."

"Well, then, I kin see there's no gonna be bloodshed, after all," Paddy said. "Come on Rosso, les' give 'em some privacy."

Rosso gave Anne a searching look, then he smiled slightly and followed Paddy up the beach. The sea whispered against the sand, a monotonous backdrop to the crunching footsteps of the two men as they walked a short distance away, talking quietly.

Anne's gaze went from Jack to Alexandra, then Charlie, then back to Jack again.

The longer the silence went on, the more nervous Jack looked. "Mama, you're not really angry, are you?" Jack said finally. "I thought..."

"Bloody hell, Jack, you take after me far too much. But it's too late to change either of us now." Anne shrugged and looked at Alexandra. "And you, you're cut from the same cloth, Alex. Damn my eyes, I don't know how you kept all this from me while sharing my own cabin." She searched Alexandra's face. "Should I be saying welcome to the family now? Or do you want the apology first? You can slap me too, if you're so inclined. I'll allow it, just the once, mind you."

Alexandra and Charlie exchanged puzzled frowns.

"I told you she'd be like this," Jack said to his sister. "She means an apology for leaving you behind when you were a babe." To Anne, he said, "Alex isn't angry with you. She only tricked you so she'd have a chance to get to know you without me around. And without you knowing who she was."

Alexandra nodded, Anne's handprint on her cheek fading. "I'm not angry. I was well-raised with the money Calico left. I had good parents. I just wanted to meet you."

"Well. That's it, then. So, you sent the note, Alex. But who's got the other half of my damned sea-glass heart?"

Charlie stuck a hand in her trouser pocket and pulled out a tiny object. "The note in the chest was mine, but I'm not good at lettering, so Jo did it for me. When Jack told us how he'd found Jo through their Da's clue, I wanted to be part o' it. Jo is the closest thing I got to family, and I got to admit, I wanted to meet the famous lady pirate, Anne Bonny." She opened up her hand, and the red sea-glass in her palm glittered in the sunlight. "Jack only took up the heart to make sure ya came after us. I'm right sorry I broke it. I made him put half with ma note in the chest."

Anne accepted the small piece of red-glass, still warm from Charlie's pocket.

Jack laughed ruefully. "I was hiding nearby, waiting for you to leave, then Sara almost caught me when I put it with the plaster in your desk."

"Ye were near during Da's funeral?" Anne asked, her brogue thickening with disapproval, "And ye didn't come and pay your respects? Jack!"

Jack flushed. "He was not a nice man and an even worse father." His lips tightened in a way that Anne recognized. She'd seen it many times when they talked about his grand-da.

"True enough, but I raised ye better'n that."

"Sorry, Mama."

It was obvious to Anne that Jack didn't really mean his apology, but she let it go. Jack and his grandfather had never gotten along, and she didn't much blame him. William Cormac had been a right bastard with everyone including his own daughter.

Alexandra stepped close enough to Charlie to sling her arm over the other young woman's shoulders, "I've known Charlie all my life. She's my sister, like you and Mary."

Charlie gave Alexandra a small smile, and in that one exchange, Anne could see the love between them. While the thought of her and Mary being sisterly struck Anne as humorous, it put her mind at rest to know that their children had grown up together. She wondered how they'd met, and how Charlie had grown up, but she had plenty of time to learn the young woman's story. Judging from how Jack's eyes kept following the young woman's every movement, she might be part of Anne's family soon.

Anne pulled the fine chain from around her neck. Dangling from a twist of wire looped onto the chain was the other half of the sea-glass heart. For a brief moment, she fit the two pieces together and then let them separate again, one in each palm. "You should have this then, the other half of my love's heart," she said, handing it to Alexandra. "Although Mary and I weren't exactly sisterly." She smiled at Jack's startled look.

"You... and Mary?" Jack said, his brow furrowing in.

Alexandra slipped the chain over her head, a few links catching in her short curls.

Anne reached out and gently detached it, so that it fell in a circle around her daughter's neck. She nodded to Jack, "Yes, we were lovers."

"I told ya so," Charlie said smugly and stuck out her hand, palm up.

Alexandra and Jack sighed and reached into their belt pouches for coins, which they each handed to Charlie.

Grinning, she tucked them away into her own belt pouch.

The red glass glimmered against the white shirt Alexandra wore. In the sunlight, Anne could see strands of auburn in the young woman's close-cropped hair. Whatever she'd used to hide her natural hair colour was fading—she'd be as red-headed as Anne within a few days.

Impulsively, she handed the second small bit of sea-glass back to Charlie. "Ye should keep this piece, Charlie. Seems only fitting that Mary's child and mine have the two halves."

Charlie grinned broadly. "I'll put it on a chain like yours, Jo."

Alexandra smiled back at the taller young woman.

Anne suddenly remembered her other question: why had Jack left Smyth in charge of the Enigma? "Jack, why are ye here?" she asked quietly.

"To meet you!" Jack replied quickly.

Too quickly, Anne thought. She gave him a stern look, and Jack quailed under it.

"I wanted to..." he trailed off.

Charlie laid a hand on his arm, "She's your mama. If anyone knows, she would."

Jack let out an explosive sigh. "Charlie thinks Calico might have left something here."

Charlie smacked his arm. "Idiot! 'Twas your idea, not mine!"

"What? You mean like buried treasure?" Alexandra asked, a gleam in her eye.

Anne chuckled. "'Twas a rare pirate tha' didn't spend all his money as he got it. Calico didn't bury nothing. Ye're wastin' yer time."

"Well, he buried something at least once," Alexandra pointed out.

Anne laughed briefly at the reminder of the plaster cast that had begun this adventure. "Ye've a point, but I was with him most o' tha time he was here, and I don't recollect him burying anythin'."

Jack got the same stubborn look on his face that Anne remembered from his childhood. "I'm going to keep looking."

Anne rolled her eyes.

Alexandra cleared her throat and changed the subject, "Are we forgiven then for tricking you?"

Anne gave her and Jack a stern look. "Not entirely, but I know what ye kin do to make it up ta me."

She was certain that none of them would be happy to hear what she had in mind, but she wasn't going to constrict her life to suit anyone else ever again. She'd done that for too many years already. She'd wrested the wheel of her own life back, and she would be damned if she gave up her Captaincy again. Not even for her children.

Hostis Humani Generis

Jack exchanged a confused look with the two young women. "Now tha' ye've all dragged me back ta sea, I don't plan ta stay on land any more than I need ta, but I don't want ta leave my children behind neither." Anne smiled at Charlie to tell her that she was included as one of Anne's children before continuing. "Even if they're full grown." She took a deep breath then continued.

"There ain't room for all o' us in me da's house even if I wanted ta go back. So, here's what I'm proposin'. We stay at sea wit' *Anne's Revenge.* While we should scuttle yer Navy ship—"

Jack gasped, and Anne held up a hand to forestall him speaking. "What if we keep usin' it as our cover? If tha *Enigma* keeps sailin' as our escort, we can stay at sea as long as we want."

"Mama, I have to give it back at some point. I never meant to take it in the first place. As long as I have that ship, the Royal Navy will never stop looking for me."

"How on God's green earth do ye accidentally steal a ship?" Anne demanded, staring hard at her son.

"I was..." Jack broke off when both Charlie and Alexandra began to snicker. His cheeks staining bright red, he glared at the young women, and they dissolved into gales of laughter.

"He was trying to protect his virtue," Alexandra gasped out when she'd regained her breath. "His Commander wanted a little rough and tumble."

Jack smacked her across the shoulder. "You didn't have to tell my mother that!"

Anne had to bite her lip to stop laughing along with the two lasses. How she had raised such a pure-minded son, she surely didn't know, but Alexandra and Charlie seemed to have a better grasp of things at least. And it appeared that Smyth had told her the truth. About this at least.

"I'm no sure how tha' leads ta stealin' a ship, Jackie, ma boy. I'll want ta hear tha whole story later."

Alexandra grinned crookedly. "If he don't tell you, I will. It's a good one."

Charlie snorted with laughter, then grew serious. "If we're gonna stay at sea, we'll need papers to hide our identities."

"I have connections in New York. We can find someone ta forge us what we need." Anne didn't entirely trust James Bonny, but she could locate other old friends who were willing to slide over the line of the law occasionally. Perhaps Jack's friend Hal Slocam could be of assistance too. If he were still friends with Jack, he'd undoubtedly have a wicked side to him, even if she hadn't seen it.

"I didn't think you'd want to go back home." Jack turned serious. "But what about Sara and George?"

"So long as I show my face there a few times a year, no one will ever know I'm gone. If I can get George settled somewhere,

Sara would be happy to join us." Anne looked around. "I'm staying at sea. Ye're all welcome to join Cap'n Mad Annie or not. But I'm never going back ta tha' mausoleum for more than a day or two here and there."

Three sets of eyes widened simultaneously. Anne chuckled at the identical looks of shock. It served them right for giving her the shock of her life today.

"We can't do that, Mama! They'll court-martial me when they catch me!"

"I'll be hanged! You wan' to be a pirate agin!"

"I'm in."

Jack and Charlie whipped around to stare at Alexandra, their mouths agape.

"I think it's a marvelous idea. We'll be together. Captain... I mean Mama..." Alexandra smiled shyly. "And I will keep you safe, Jackie-boy. It's perfect."

Anne clapped a hand on Alexandra's shoulder with a broad grin. "That's me lass." A shiver of pleasure at those words filled her.

Charlie and Jack began arguing again, but Anne left it to Alexandra to argue back. She'd wait until their arguments dried up before she said her piece. She had plans. First stop would be to New York to make further arrangements with James Bonny. And then north to the French island to see if she could find Eusebe Bernard, the remarkable blacksmith she kept hearing about. She stroked the long dagger hanging at her waist. With more of these, her crew would be unstoppable.

A large hand touched down on her shoulder, and she turned to see Rosso grinning at her. She smiled back.

"Ya'll have me in your crew, where e'er ya go," he said quietly.

Taking his arm, Anne walked a short distance onto the firm wet sand to look out to sea where their two ships bobbed in the waves. The white canvas sails shone in the sunlight, and she momentarily wished she could fly her new flag. She had never truly considered sinking either of them for more than a brief moment—their cover story of merchantman and escort was far too useful for the future she had in mind. She sat in the hot sand and pulled Rosso down to sit beside her, so close their thighs were almost touching. The heat of the sand was welcome under her aching hip.

Rosso cleared his throat. "Ya sure ya want to do this? Ya'd be paintin' a target on ya back."

She didn't hesitate even a moment. "I'm tired of pretendin' ta be Anne Cormac, the respectable widow and landlubber. With tha *Enigma* by our side, we're going ta have some easy pickings. And maybe I wouldn't mind helpin' a few times along the way, like we did with Rosie and Capulet." A shiver of relief ran up her backbone at finally sharing her dreams with someone else.

Rosso laughed, a huge belly laugh. "Don't kid yourself. Ya ain't doing this for anyone else. Ya just wanna be a pirate, again."

She winked at him, remembering the phrase Henry had quoted during the trial. *Hostis Humani Generis:* it meant an enemy of mankind, but it was frequently used to mean a gentleman of fortune, or lady of fortune, in her case. "O' course! I ain't dead, and I'm no gonna let meself be buried alive in that house anymore." She half turned to face him and stroked his forearm. The hair rose up in response. "You know the bloom ain't off me rose."

"Cap'n..."

"I know what people will say!" she snapped, "I don't care—they ain't tha ones with tha itch."

"So, I'm an itch?" The tightness in his voice could have been annoyance, but she was willing to bet he was trying not to laugh.

"Mebbe. And mebbe it's both of us with an itch." She grinned. "When we're alone, I'd ask tha' ye call me Anne."

He looked around, and then, with a slow smile, he nodded without quite meeting her eyes. "Anne. I might have an itch too."

The heat in his voice made the hairs on her arms rise up. Anne glanced over her shoulder at Jack, Alexandra, and Charlie, still arguing vehemently, arms waving to emphasize some point or other. She squeezed Rosso's arm and settled back into the sand, perfectly content to sit quietly with him and contemplate the future.

Behind her, Alexandra laughed at something Jack said. She sounded very much like Calico when she laughed. Anne thought Calico would have been happy to meet the lass—she was brash like both her parents, bright like her brother, and had the heart of a pirate.

A small wave washed higher onto the beach, flicking salty droplets onto her bare feet. Anne sighed happily. She had her children, maybe a new lover, and a bonny vessel.

It was good to be out of hiding.

ᴀCKNOWLEDGEMENTS

I'd like to thank Ontario Arts Council's Recommender Grants for supporting the creation of this book, and particularly Second Story Press for recommending my project. The encouragement upon receiving a grant is incalculable. Thank you to The Speculative Literature Foundation, particularly Malon Edwards. I didn't receive a grant, but your encouraging comments kept me believing in it.

I'd like to thank the many readers and writers that have read various drafts of this story as it went from a short story to a novella to a novel: Emily Ramsay, Julie Cullen, Barbara Kwasniewski, Nemma Wollenfang, Kris Ramsay, Sandra Marcroft, Donna Thiel Cook, and Elaine Chen. Your comments were astute and helped make this tale what it is now.

A special thank you to the people who encouraged me to write—some of whom read early drafts of this novel—the Bloor West Writers gang: Maaja Wentz, Rebecca Simkin, Bryan Dawes, Cai Guise-Richardson, Kimberley Fehr, Lisa Wilder, Sameh Gabarin, Alexandre Leger, Christine Vasilevski, Pam

Ferguson, Marianne Miller, Ann Dulhanty, Doris Muise, Ken Leland, Gillian Kerr, Peter Timmerman, Sten Eirik, Jim Moore, and Alison Gadsby. You all made a decade's worth of Thursday night escapes from my kids special.

I read a great many books and websites as I researched the 1700s, ranging from ship descriptions, prices of common goods, blacksmithing, historical events, popular culture, and fun euphemisms for sex. There are far too many sources to list here, but any mistakes are mine alone.

ABOUT THE AUTHOR

Carolyn Charron is a speculative fiction writer who has always wanted to be a pirate or a wizard, preferably with a dragon companion. Her short stories have appeared in Renaissance Press's *Nothing Without Us,* an anthology of disabled writers, which was nominated for a 2020 Prix Aurora Award, and in three of Flame Tree Publishing's Gothic Fantasy anthologies among others. On the editor's side of her desk, she read slush for *Apex, Lightspeed,* and *Nightmare* magazines, and has been a juror for Speculative Literature Foundation grants.

She was fortunate to receive a Recommender Grant from Ontario Arts Council (OAC) to write this novel, the prequel to a multigenerational series of stories following a family of blacksmiths and their magical power over metals. The next novel has also received both OAC Recommender grants and a Toronto Arts Council grant.

She lives in Toronto with her husband and two children and is still hoping for a pet dragon one day.

IRIS and the CREW TEAR THROUGH SPACE!
by Cait Gordon

In a galactic network known as the Keangal, where space is accessible...Lieutenant Eileen Iris and the command crew of the *S.S. SpoonZ* haven't a clue what it means to be disabled. An unexpected conversation with an intergalactic janitor brings up the question but offers no answers before he's 'ported away. Unfazed, duties resume as Iris manages an overprotective guidebot; Security Chief Lartha and her sentient prostheses offer kick-ass protection; Mr. Herbert's inventiveness is a godsend (although he's not quite grasped how to flirt); Commander Davan's affable personality comes through whether trumpeted, texted, or signed; and Captain Warq's gracious but firm leadership keeps everyone at their best. Until on one mission, where the crew tears through space.

Just a little bit.